# Shadow of Desire

By

## Aila Awatt

# Dedication

Thanks for reading. Mystery and desire make for the perfect combination.

# Chapter One

Looking up into the sky there were several different planes landing in different sections of the airport. The one we had been waiting for pulled up to the runway. Refraining from waving I knew I would only look crazy waving at a plane that no one could see me. I couldn't exactly explain the fact I was able to see the passengers sitting in their seats still wearing their seatbelts. As it pulled up to the airport. I could feel myself getting jittery except when I tried to contain my excitement. I might have been this excited to see her, but she might not feel the same way, not that it would have helped me any.

"Do you think she'll remember me?" Gregory asked.

"Are you crazy? Skylar has only been gone for one year finishing up her internship, if she forgot who you are then she would have amnesia. Why not tell her how you feel about her?" Michael asked.

"I swear her internship was far too long. Mine only lasted three months and I did mine here. Besides, you know why I can't." Gregory sounded serious and sad at the same time.

"If you know you'll never allow yourself to have a relationship with her then why torture yourself like this? Why be this close to her if you're only going to keep hurting yourself. Yeah, she's a great friend but move past it." Michael stated.

"I've had a crush on her ever since kindergarten when I let her take my toys from me, all through life we've been best friends and even when I made sure she was late going to the prom because of that night, she'll never know the real reason I was late and she can't know, not even enough to know why her date never showed up. At this point she would think I was clinically insane. I don't want to be away from her, I can't stop protecting her knowing what's out there." Gregory stated plainly.

"What if Skylar wants a relationship with you, and then what are you going to do?" Michael asked.

"I would be the happiest and most destroyed man in the world.

Perhaps it's time I spend less time with her, that way when I'm no longer around she won't give it a second thought. I can still keep her safe from a distance." Gregory said.

"For now, let's concentrate on welcoming her home. She's heading right over here now." Michael said as he walked past me to greet her.

I looked at her the same way I had for our entire life, which hadn't really been very long but after certain events. I knew mine was going to be long, one not even I could put a timeline on. There was a reason Michael had known, not because of being my best friend and my little brother. He had been there, and I was the reason they never had a chance to get at him. For most high school students who were getting ready for the prom, dancing and music. I had other plans, at least ones that were thrown at me. My brother Michael had been waiting around for his friends, one in particular. Since others liked to pick on him. He was one of the sweetest kids and sadly one of the most vulnerable so as a loyal brother he waited for his last friend to show. When he wasn't coming, he went looking for him. The two of us walked along the path he normally took, not really wanting a car Carson walked a lot.

We didn't have to get very far before we heard his voice scream for help. He was lying on the ground with four taller and much bigger guys over him kicking him. One was standing back laughing as if he was entertained by harming another person. Both Michael and I had taken off in their direction determined to stop them even if we had been outnumbered. Fighting might not have been my thing to do but I couldn't ever stand by watching a friend get beat up or bullied. I had tackled the two from behind while Michael took out the other two on the side. From the corner of my eye, I could see Michael using the fighting styles he was taught in class, I always wanted to make sure he could protect himself if I wasn't around. A mixture of street fighting and jiu-jitsu. I always marveled at how well he had taken to it except I couldn't get this sound out of my head. Once I had my opponent on the ground I tried to locate it. Once I had I couldn't believe it. Here were two of them making almost a humming growl sound in unison and I wasn't sure what was about to happen until I had seen them show their teeth.

Once Carson was standing and next to Michael, I noticed the other guys were already fleeing almost as if they knew what was going to happen. Turning to my brother, normally I would say one thing, run, and I knew he trusted what I was doing. We always talked about if something happened it was easier if I protected myself than to worry if he was safe, to get out of the way and find a safe place until I could get to him.

"I knew I didn't need to say anything else, that Michael would get Carson out of here and to a safer place. He knew I would catch up with both of them soon. After I said these words, they took off in a hurry knowing our rule except what I hadn't known is that I wouldn't see either of them for over a week.

I might have been a good fighter but the first few attacks I hadn't seen coming. I felt my skin burn and could feel the trickling of blood all over my body so that I was beginning to think I wasn't going to survive this. My thoughts were not how would I survive but if I died, there would be no one to protect my brother and his friend. It seemed like there were more here than before as I looked around and barely saw the shadows of the others around me. I don't know why they didn't fight us like this before unless they had to lose their temper or were not expecting us to challenge them. I barely moved before I was flung through the air like a rag doll hitting the tree. What scared me even more than the pain I was in, had been the tormented screaming and thunderous boom. My eyes were far too swollen shut to see what was going on. Then the truly scary moment when everything went silent. Were they leaving me for dead or did something else happen that I wasn't aware of?

Something lifted me up off the ground cradling me as the wind rushed around us. My vision was already bad, but I was sure the world around me was flying by. I could hear a door open and next thing I knew; my clothes were being torn off me and I was placed in cold water. It felt like a shock, but I was also not used to being handled by someone else, someone I didn't even know, or I might have if I could see them. They were being careful but using a washcloth cleaning over my cuts. They were not discreet about where they touched me, but nothing seemed like it was done to be sexual but simply to clean me. There were several times my body felt like it erupted in heat, they hadn't added anything hot, but it felt like my entire body was on fire. The person added ice cubes, but they would melt each time I had a flair up. Letting the water out of the tub, they lifted me and laid me on a bed, drying me off, putting clothing on me and then they left me laying there on the bed alone to finish the healing on my own. They never came back, and I hadn't found out who they were.

To this day I didn't know if they were still around, if I was a vampire, werewolf or something else. I felt like a monster and didn't risk spending too much time around others in case my inner demon decided to come out. All I knew was when it did, I wasn't conscious of it, almost as if I blacked out when it happened. One of the reasons I was afraid to get involved with any relationship, especially with the girl I loved.

I felt a slap on the back of the head as I looked over slightly and saw her standing there smiling at me with a smile I grew to love. I realized I was lost in my own thoughts, and she slapped me as she had many times when we were kids.

"What were you dreaming about this time? It must have been good since I slapped you twice" Skylar gave me a huge hug.

"It wasn't important, how was your flight, obviously it was good since you made it home." I felt like an idiot asking such a mundane question.

"It wasn't bad, but I am happy to be back home and done with school for now. I have two weeks before I start working, I accepted the administration job at the hospital. Has anything changed while I was gone," Skylar looked at both of us, "don't tell me nothing happened while I was gone, you two are always getting into something."

"It was rather slow, I dated a few people, Gregory lived like a hermit in his cottage, we spent a little time at the bar but nothing exciting. Unless of course you count the black bear, who came through, grabbing food from one of the tables and leaving with it, other than that not much changes out here. I was surprised you took the job here; I thought living in a large city might have been more exciting for you." Micheal voiced what we both thought might happen.

"I loved the city, but it can be exhausting, besides I couldn't wait to get back to my own home and privacy. It was great but nothing beats coming home. If you both want to go to the bar tomorrow night, I promised Camden we could spend some time together tonight, I haven't seen him for a while and he's leaving tomorrow now that his internship was accepted." Giving us both a hug, we started to walk towards our car.

"I know we are both happy to have you back home." Micheal got into the driver's seat.

I opened the door for Skylar as I insisted on sitting in the backseat. Our ride to her home was rather quiet as she spoke about her experience and what she had been busy doing. I kept thinking over in my thoughts, if she meant so much to Camden, why wasn't he here picking her up? I was thankful we did, I always loved seeing her. After dropping her off, giving her one last hug before confirming we would take her out to the bar the next night. It felt strange leaving her there when normally we all would have hung out, but I knew it was because of her boyfriend.

"I know that look in your eyes, your obsessed with her, tell her how you feel." Micheal jabbed me slightly as I got into the front seat.

"You know I can't, you're the only one who knows and it's going to stay that way. Drop me off at my car, I'm not exactly in the mood to go out tonight." I knew I couldn't fight my own bad mood that I put myself into.

"As you wish but I'm pretty sure I'll be seeing you later." Micheal stayed quiet until he dropped me off.

I sat in my car for a while trying to convince myself that I should go home but I kept wanting to make sure she was safe even if she was with her boyfriend. As I drove, I went past my home and kept going, I knew it was a bad idea, but I still did it anyway. Parking down the road slightly I made my way through the woods. I wasn't worried if she let her dog out which I'm sure he's happy she's finally home. I had dropped him off at her house earlier this morning after caring for him while she was gone. She called him on the phone every day just to talk to him, she was worried he would forget who she was and didn't want to risk leaving, it was the reason she said she wasn't going to get her medical PhD, so I had to talk her into going. It's weird to think she's a doctor now, or at least closer, there were still classes she needed to take.

I loved the bay windows of her home, living in the woods might not give a person all the privacy they might think, especially when everything in your home is on display. I knew I shouldn't be out here watching her. I kept telling myself it was to keep her safe but part of me felt jealous that it should have been me in there with her. This was a person she dated for a while. During the time she was gone for her internship, he was seeing other girls, not that she seemed to be worried about it. He dropped his clothes on the living room floor and started a fire in the fireplace. He was tall with a medium muscular frame, dark brown wavy hair, piercing blue eyes, he never had a problem getting a girl to look in his direction. He laid down on the plush rug while she put her clothes on the couch near him and sat down leaning against him.

It might have been my opinion or guilty pleasure, but she was the most beautiful women to me. Fiery red long hair to her waist that matched her personality, adventurous, and intelligent. She was a little on the shorter side with curves that I wanted to run my hands along. Her dark green eyes were mesmerizing. I watched from a distance as she ran her fingers through his chest hair. Slowly she ran her fingers down his stomach until she was down by his crotch, playfully teasing him, caressing his legs and getting incredibly close. She moved over to sit on top of him, positioning his penis, pressing it against the opening. He tried to push upward as she moved and prevented him from entering.

I couldn't help but think, way to go, you stopped him even though

I knew it was eventually going to happen. I was tempted to call her on the phone to interrupt but I remembered she always said she left the phone turned off.

I watched as she placed her hands on his chest and sat down rather quickly, as he put his hands on her hips pulling her more onto him. sliding up and down on his penis a couple times before she grinded on him, sliding her hips forward and back. Leaning over occasionally to kiss him on the lips. From this angle I could see her breasts move until he kept holding onto her, then he rolled them both over and he was now laying on top of her. I could barely see her other than her hands holding onto his hips, he would move upward slightly pivoting his hips back and forth.

"I can't believe you're watching her have sex, if you are so damn jealous, then go talk to her but this is sick watching her through her window have sex with another guy." Micheal seemed to be surprised as he came over to kneel next to me.

"You're in the same boat, you're out here watching her also, what does that make you?" I challenged.

"We all know I'm perverted. If there is a free show, I'm either watching or participating in it. I'm not trying to convince myself I'm not interested. Now that he's on top there isn't much to watch." Micheal said as he got up and left me there.

When I saw her gripping his hips with her hands, I knew she didn't need me. I made my way out of the woods carefully and back to my car. I don't know why I tortured myself like that, why watch when I know nothing with us was going to happen. We kissed once but that was it. We've always been extremely close, almost inseparable when we were kids. Now that she was back, I desperately needed a hobby and drinking wasn't going to be it again, I can't go down that road again, it didn't help. I thought caring for her dog kept my mind off her but not that well, hearing her voice every night she called Taffy, and the fact I knew I had her dog, which got me to thinking, I'll go to the county over and get a dog, it can't hurt. Before I realized I was already home, parking beside my house and up to the front door, there was a note left for me. No name to say who it was from other than the letter E on one side. Pulling the paper from the door and unfolding it. The words inside were short and not much explanation other than, "at night only." That didn't make much sense. Looking around hoping something else might have been left but nothing was changed, moved or any other notes to be seen. Unlocking the door. I let myself in and decided not to worry about it.

# Chapter Two

I was thankful I had the next three weeks off even though it would have been a great distraction. I wasn't good at taking time off, Micheal had to argue for his time off, my boss threatened to fire me if I didn't take it soon. So, I stayed home, and I had been building a large glass aviary, which I originally thought of keeping birds and various plants until I remembered most birds hated me and I didn't like cleaning up after them. I kept the outside structure and dug a huge hole. There was enough space along the sides for a walkway where I could place lounge chairs to relax on and the hole became my knew swimming pool. It was a mixture of pool and natural plants that organically filtered the water. I was always obsessed with the waterfall grotto style, so I made sure the far end was fitted with one. It took me the entire year Skylar was gone to build this. I could have had it done earlier but I was to much of a perfectionist, that and playing with Taffy took up my time.

Getting dressed for this evening, I wanted to look my best, and even if he was there, I wanted to welcome my best friend back the right way. Leaving the house, I found a sticky note on my windshield. It read 'caves' and that was all. I was curious who was doing this but if they were messing with me or sending a secret message, I wasn't getting it. Crumbling it up and hitting the side of the trash can, I picked it up and put it inside the can. My truck was getting fixed, so I drove to the bar in my little car, I lived a little closer, so it hadn't taken long, the parking lot was rather full this evening. Skylar parked near Micheal's car, always in the far corner of the parking lot.

It was a small bar; they were more of a small diner with any drink you hoped they could make. The food was amazing which is why I rarely ate at home. At least one of the reasons, mainly that I hated doing dishes so if I could avoid it, I did. Micheal waved for me to join them in the corner. There were a couple of our friends and Skylar had an open seat next to her. I looked around but hadn't seen Camden.

"Is this seat taken?" I assumed he would be sitting next to her.

"It's open for you. Camden is at home." Skylar had a quick drink.

"Did something happen?" Micheal sounded confused.

"We had a great evening and while he was in the kitchen this morning, I was sent a bunch of photos showing what he's been busy doing this last year. Or rather what he had been on top of. I confronted him about it, and he said, since we were not married, he could sleep with anyone he wanted. So, I broke up with him. I don't need someone around I can't trust, it's one thing if he had been honest but to think he's the only one who can see others, that I'm not allowed and to bring people back to my home without my permission, then yes, it's over." Skylar hadn't sounded upset at all.

"Do you want to talk about this or get wasted and forget it ever happened?" Micheal asked curiously.

"I should be upset but I think I kind of knew before I left. I don't know but it's weird, I should be upset for being cheated on, sex last night was great, but it was more the pleasure than anything, other than that, I felt nothing for him. what I do want to do is have some fun but the kind I'll remember." Skylar slightly glanced at me as she grabbed my hand pulling me out into the middle of the room.

Micheal started up the old music box and a few other couples joined us. There was a small dance floor in the far back part of the bar where they rented it out for parties or receptions. The selection of music wasn't great but there were a few that always put us in the mood to dance, it was one of those few times you had an excuse to touch each other and move around the dance floor.

After dancing for a while, we sat back down with the drinks that we ordered. I hadn't though anything of it until I went to put my cup back down onto the coaster, other than the company logo, there was a small sticky note with one word written with the same handwriting as the others, it said, 'tonight.' Picking it up I looked it over, it was closer to the first one, I was curious who E was.

"Do either of you know anything about this or have you seen it before? I had a note on my house door, then on my windshield and now on the coaster." It seemed strange since we were all together so I knew it couldn't be my brother or Skylar.

"Only person around the table was the waitress, we were all dancing and the table was empty." Skylar waved down the waitress to come over.

"Did you need anything else?" She asked kindly.

"My friend was left a sticky note, we were wondering if you saw who left it?" Skylar asked.

"A young woman came in and asked me to put it on the coaster for you, she said she was a friend who couldn't stick around but needed to give you an answer to something." The waitress waited to see if we needed anything else.

"What did she look like?" I was curious if I could guess.

"She was a young lady, long blonde hair to her waist, a few braids going down the back almost like a net design, it was very pretty. Unfortunately, I didn't pay attention to her clothing color other than jeans and a shirt. I did notice she had piercing blue eyes, that would be difficult to forget." As we thanked her, she left our table.

"I can't think of anyone like that, and I don't know how the E helps any. I'm guessing they want to meet me at the caves tonight at night, but that's a bit strange to meet someone I don't know and who knows what time tonight. I'm not going to mess with it, if its someone I know they will say something but since they are not, I don't trust them." My comment was true, but I had to admit to myself I was curious, it was the sort of trouble Skylar usually expected Micheal and I to get into.

"I don't think it would be safe going around trying to find this person, if they wanted to be found they would have been clearer. I think they are just messing with you." Skylar looked concerned.

"Should we make this a threesome and check it out together?" Micheal smiled as he said it.

"Never say threesome when it involves your brother and you, no we should not check it out." Skylar shuddered at the thought of doing something with Micheal.

"I'm heading home tonight, nothing good ever happens after three in the morning. Plus, I plan on picking up a dog from the shelter, I admit I was spoiled taking care of Taffy while you were gone." I was getting used to the idea of having a pet and looked forward to it.

"Make sure you get one that Taffy will get along with, that way they can have playdates and if either of us go anywhere we know they will get along. I'm not doing anything in the morning, I could come with you and bring Taffy?" Skylar looked excited at the idea.

"That sounds good, with my luck I couldn't pick, and I might bring them all home." I was thankful our food was brought to us; I had hoped to pick out an animal to get my mind off of Skylar.

After a few more hours, Skylar was the first to go, Micheal kept trying to hint towards checking out the mysterious notes, he was always up for good mystery. I waited back for a reason, if this was something bad, it was easier watching after myself than being worried if something happened to anyone else. If they had seen anything on my car they would have brought it into me. When I made my way to my car, there it was, a small sticky note on my windshield. I looked around to see if the person hung around to find out if I got it. I hadn't seen anyone. The note read, "I know who changed you."

I found myself holding the note a little tighter, no one else should have known, could this be who saved me after I was attacked? I highly doubted it was the direct source of who did this, it was a young man who bullied us, but a couple years later, I know he died in a fire, not sure how or why it started. Even the authorities were confused but they found his body burned and identified it as him and the person leaving the notes was female. Did this person intend on blackmailing me over it? I never wanted anyone else to know, people react strangely and out of fear of something they don't understand, they lash out without thinking, even though I haven't hurt anything my entire life.

Being paranoid, I looked over my car and around the engine, I wasn't very trustful of people especially those who didn't tell me who they were and what they wanted from me. It wasn't too late yet, but I knew where they wanted to meet me, at least I hoped it was the same caves that I thought it might be, there were not that many near here. The long winding road soon turned into a seasonal road which didn't get much attention, it desperately needed to be grated, the road was bumpy and full of huge potholes. Driving along the edge being careful, I followed it until there was a divider with three different possible directions. I knew my car would never make it through the soft sand. I missed my truck, but I should be getting it back soon, not that it helped me right now, otherwise I would have drove that through here with no problems.

Getting out and picking the path to the right, I walked down towards the rocky side along to the beach. It was easier there until it curved and no longer had an easy footpath. There was a slight curve in the rocks where I climbed up, in the short distance there was an opening to the cave, thankfully the water has never entered the cave but does cover the rocks outside sometimes making them slippery. I hadn't seen anything to indicate anyone around. Watching the ground and above to make sure nothing was going to drop down on me, I entered the cave.

I could have used my flashlight since it's usually dark in here, but it was rather well lit with torches lining the walls. They were rather intricately designed black iron webbing holding each torch in place, a total of eight, four on each side.

Towards the back there was a marble green piece of furniture, fashioned for relaxation, lying invitingly in the center of the dimly lit room. Its surface was perfectly flat yet designed to allow a person to recline at an angle that suggested both comfort and restraint, with shimmering chains affixed at each corner like an alluring invitation. Accompanying this intriguing piece was a note that cryptically instructed me to lie down upon its cool surface, secure myself with the blindfold provided, and fasten the chains around my wrists as if embracing some hidden thrill. The idea sent a shiver down my spine; I could feel my heart racing as I contemplated these instructions. After all, how could I even think about obeying such strange demands without knowing who orchestrated this unsettling scene or what their true intentions might be? What was worse, I felt temporarily turned on by it. Shaking my head, I swear. I'll be the cause to my own ending, and I wondered how Skylar could risk dating strangers and taking them home.

I sat on the ground for a while as I watched the sun go down, it was complete darkness outside, looking around I wondered if the person could see me, but I hadn't seen anything that looked like a camera. Wanting to speed up the process, I laid down on the marble green slab with the shape of a body that fit snugly to me. I laid the chains over my wrists and laid the blindfold over my eyes but hadn't fastened any of them. I could hear a slight crunch now that I had done this. I hoped once they were close enough, I could surprise them by jumping up and seeing who it was.

That's when they gave me the surprise, the chains clicked shut around my ankles and wrists, the blindfold slid behind my head fastening itself. Someone was using magic I hadn't witnessed before. Now I was at their mercy.

"Whose there? I can hear you, why so much secrecy if you supposedly know something about me?" I hoped they would answer.

"I haven't decided if I wish for you to know who I am yet." The voice sounded feathery light, definitely no one I knew.

"How long do you think you can keep me here? I have friends who will come look for me if I don't show up later." I wasn't sure how well this person knew me.

"You mean your brother Micheal and Skylar. You're not much for making friends, if you had then this would have been much easier. That route hadn't worked so I had to try a second way of getting to you, your always around those two." She was walking around me as air slightly breezed past.

"You have me, now what do you want with me? Doesn't tying me up seem a bit dramatic?" I doubted I was that difficult to speak with.

She hadn't spoken again but I kept feeling my shirt being pulled at. Then she tore my shirt open, running her fingers over my chest.

"He left his mark on you and yet you cannot even see it yourself." She laughed slightly.

"You just destroyed my favorite shirt, it had buttons, you could have just unbuttoned it instead of making it useless." I wore this shirt because I knew it was Skylar's favorite aqua blue color.

"I don't care about your favorite shirt, hopefully these pants are not your favorite either," She cut several areas and was able to pull them off, only the boxer briefs had been left.

"If you wanted to see me naked, I could have posed for you." I said sarcastically.

"You have no idea what he left on you so many years ago." She ran her fingers over my legs.

"I'm pretty sure whatever you think was left on me was showered off years ago, my mother was meticulous at having us bathe to get clean." I wished I knew what she was looking for or at.

"This cannot be washed off. The idiot was simply going to kill you, but our leader felt you could do great things someday, he was so wrong trusting a human simpleton." She sounded disgusted.

"Mind telling me what he did, if he had his way with my body while I was unconscious, I'm not going to pretend to like that. I don't mind others who do but I don't swing that way." I wasn't worried about upsetting her.

"If he so desired, there was literally nothing stopping him from doing absolutely anything your body could possibly handle, but instead of opting for the more traditional approaches to chaos and mischief, he chose to intricately inscribe these ancient runes into your skin— symbols that hold the weight of our legendary tales, hidden secrets, fervent desires, and untold power. It's a marvel how someone as delightfully clueless as you came to possess such astonishing potential; honestly, it's like watching a goldfish trying to do calculus!" She laughed as she tried to insult me.

"I assume you want these symbols. I would assume it doesn't quite work as easily as removing someone's flesh." I hoped it wasn't what she hoped to do, I liked the way my skin looked on me.

"They can only be extracted by the one who created them, but they might pass on." She positioned herself over me as I could feel her skin against mine." She leaned forward sniffing my skin.

It didn't take her long to cut my brief and remove it. I felt it as she pulled it away throwing it somewhere. At least now I can understand why I found underwear by the beach at times, gross, but makes sense.

"I'll make this work." She mumbled.

"I'm pretty sure if having sex with someone would pass it on, it's been done long ago. I don't sleep with many, but I don't turn down the opportunity often. Mind putting a condom on me? I don't know where you've been." I had a feeling I knew where this was going.

I wished I could see what the person looked like. The description sounded interesting from the waitress, that is if it happened to be the same person. But I always preferred seeing the person I was going to have sex with.

"Out of all the people wandering around in this dusty little town, with its endless supply of quirky characters and charm to spare, did he seriously have to settle on you? It's not like you were competing for some kind of 'last one standing' award! There were plenty of folks he encountered whose entries into the afterlife might have been remembered more fondly—people who could've saved their loved ones a good deal of heartache if they'd just taken the plunge. But nooo, here you are—an arrogant buffoon with a penchant for trouble—instead enjoying this relentless second chance at life while others stand by wondering what makes you so special. So really, out of everyone else creeping along these dusty streets where tumbleweeds seem to mock your choices, what was it about you that earned such an improbable reprieve from eternal rest?" She sounded frustrated.

"What can I say, I'm likeable?" I always thought I got along with everyone; I still couldn't figure out who she was.

"Not by everyone." She tugged at his penis slightly.

She positioned herself over his penis, sliding it back and forth teasing him making Gregory wonder when she was going to take the plunge.

"If you unchained me, I could help you with that. We could both indulge in the intoxicating pleasure of our bodies pressed so closely together. Unless, of course, you're afraid I might seize that moment to make my escape." I was curious how far she was going with this.

"Your boundless arrogance is truly astonishing; if I so desired, I could articulate my wishes with such precision that every action you take would fall under my control. I harbor no fear of you—not even the mere thought of your potential escape dares to cross my mind—because deep down, I know that the insatiable hunger for more will inevitably draw you back into my grasp. You may think yourself free, but it is only a matter of time before you return to me once again, compelled by forces beyond your understanding." She squeezed her legs tighter against his.

Trying a little sarcasm, "I must confess, I'm feeling quite a spark of attraction towards you, and it's difficult to ignore. You're welcome to explore any desires or whims you have in mind when it comes to my anatomy—just promise me one thing: please don't go breaking anything down there! After all, I'll definitely be needing it again for future escapades and adventures." I was enjoying our back-and-forth banter.

She might have appeared to be crazy to someone else, but she had me interested now and much more curious what her future plans were, she was right I might want more. She positioned directly over my penis and dropped down quickly. Tipping her pelvis slightly. At first, she slowly rocked her hips back and forth until she started more of a rhythmic motion moving faster. Placing her hands on my chest, I could feel her nails dig in and slide down from the shoulders, along the chest and all the way down to the lower belly. It felt like water dripping until I realized it was blood.

"Am I to be your sacrifice?" I was beginning to wonder as my flesh started to feel like it was burning.

"Shut up, anything I do to you his runes heal you. I don't understand it, you heal like one of them, but you bleed like the others." She stated.

"So, no foreplay? I'm always being told women want foreplay." I was hoping to find something out about her.

"I'm here for one thing only, foreplay isn't needed, or I would be soaping you up in the shower, the foreplay you do, the whole feather sliding along a naked body isn't liked by everyone, change it up once in a while, get a little aggressive." She sounded frustrated.

"Did we actually go on a date, I have a personal rule of three, three dates and then sex. It's difficult to imagine not recognizing someone as irresistibly sexy scunding as you? Honestly, even though I'm currently blindfolded and unable to see your smile, I'm convinced that I would remember having sex with someone who can take charge let alone get me tied up."

"Gregory. Don't think too hard you were not exactly memorable. You'll only give yourself a headache." She sounded frustrated.

She placed her nails again making another line next to the others. More blood dripped but didn't last long. She gripped my sides holding on tighter as she continued. She kept arching her hips moving faster until I could feel her legs tighten around me, resting her head on my chest. She sat there for a few minutes before climbing down off from me. She hadn't removed the blindfold or chains yet. I could hear her walking around even though the sound started to get lighter.

"Do you want my phone number? Call me." I yelled as I guessed she had left.

I started to feel extremely cold. I could pull at the chains, usually I could break something like this. From when I was changed, I found I was unusually strong, I already knew I didn't bleed long. I rarely went to the hospital, or I would have had to explain why a gaping hole closed on its own without stitches, not that I knew how to explain it, I didn't understand it myself. I could hear things from miles away. I was strong, fast, intelligent even though I like to think I was smart before the change. I could daydream and certain things would happen. I had premonitions and occasionally could see through certain types of metals, like the airplane earlier. My premonitions were rather strong and rarely wrong. It was things that hadn't happened yet, but I knew a few minutes before, and it was exactly as I would see it. I tried explaining it to my brother once and he was the one who explained to me what that ability was. I was never good at labeling things. I was disappointed I didn't get to turn into a wolf or fly off as a bat. Micheal called it a gift, I called it a curse, if I dated anyone, I would see them dying, that's when I stopped dating and I didn't have those visions anymore.

I was beginning to think whoever went for an innocent stroll the beach during the day would either view themselves as either lucky or unlucky to see a naked man laying here, if I was lucky, they might be good looking and pleasure me. As I humored myself with this, the chains clinked to the ground and the blindfold let go. Sitting up and looking around, I was thankful it was still dark out. I had to walk back to my car with no clothing since she cut all of them.

# Chapter Three

Skylar asked, "where did you get those scratch marks?" Sounding concerned.

Looking down at his chest closing the top button, "wild animal."

"Was it a bear? Those need to be treated or you'll either get infected or a scar." Skylar wanted to look closer until I closed my shirt more.

"No bear, I'm not sure what it was, not to worry, I've cleaned it and removed the animal. Nothing to worry about. I'm just happy you're here to help me pick out an animal." I opened the door to the facility hoping she wouldn't ask any more questions.

"I can't help it, but you seem different?" Skylar kept watching as I walked past to go near the animals.

"In what way?" I didn't feel different, taking a quick sniff of my armpit, at least that wasn't it.

"Yep, in that way you are the same." Skylar laughed as she bent lower to look at one of the dogs in the pen.

To the right of the facility were the cats and to the left were the dogs, we didn't need directions as Taffy led us towards the dogs. Taffy had been excited to see all the dogs, there were a few that scared her, but she made it known there was a dog in the corner she was drawn to. She pressed her head against the gate door as the other dog did the same.

"I think we found my new family member." Looking at Skylar, she seemed happy with the pick.

We went to the desk with the volunteer there. Setting the phone down she asked, "did you find one you were interested in? we have a few pieces of paper for you to fill out first." She handed me three pieces of paper.

"I can fill these out for you, go show her the dog you want." Skylar said as she pulled a pen out.

We walked down the short distance, the dog Taffy picked

happened to be halfway down. Looking at the sad dog who sat in the corner, she slowly came to the door again once Taffy leaned against it.

"She's such a timid dog, there are others here who have much more energy. The one to the left is great for road trips." The volunteer thought she was pointing out something I would like.

"This one here is absolutely perfect, I trust Taffy's choice when it comes to getting along with other animals." I smiled back and was determined.

"There's a stipulation with this one and it's usually why no one wants her. She was brought in with her fees already paid for, but you must take the cat that was in the home she grew up in also." She sounded like this was a bad thing.

We walked over to where the cats were being kept, nowhere near the front, she led me to the furthest back part of the room and through another door. The volunteer stepped aside and gave into a shiver.

"We call him the cat from hell, he's attacked every volunteer here, he's not friendly at all." As she looked the cat's eyes narrowed.

Within a uniquely designed enclosure, there resided a hairless cat—not of the Egyptian breed—but rather one that exhibited an unmistakably irritable demeanor. This unusually hefty feline had narrowed eyes that conveyed an intense frustration, giving it an appearance that was both striking and somewhat menacing. Its expression seemed to suggest a perpetual state of annoyance, as if it were perpetually displeased with its surroundings and the world at large. But who could blame it after losing its home and family ending up in a somewhat sterile cage.

"I'm going to take this as a challenge, I'll be happy to take both. Maybe when he's not so stressed, his fur will grow back." I wasn't sure but couldn't hurt, he looked the way I would feel if I was stuck living here in a cage.

Two more volunteers helped get the cat moved into my car, they seemed to be happy he was leaving and not because he finally has a home. The dog perked up as she realized she was leaving the facility and getting into the car. Now the difficult part would be naming it, something I was never good at, if Skylar suggested something, I was going to use it.

There was another note on my car, grabbing it before Skylar saw it, I definitely didn't want to discuss last night, if she asked again, she had a way of getting the truth out of me and I didn't want her telling me how incredibly stupid I was for playing along last night, even though I did get turned on and enjoyed some of it. I realize it could have gone horribly wrong.

"I'll bring Taffy over tomorrow afternoon. I have a blind date tonight. Did you pick a name for her yet or the cat? I'm still surprised you took him; he looks so ornery." The cat hissed at her when Skylar mentioned him.

"They came as a pair, I don't mind, I'm sure he'll calm down once he feels safe. On the paper it said their former owner passed away and his name was listed as Otis, so I'm going to keep that. They had her name listed as 'dog', I'm pretty sure she knows she is one so I might change it to Honey, Coco, Peaches or Nibbles?" I was never good with names.

"I think you're hungry, go eat and name her after or you could name her Clover." Skylar sounded hopeful.

"I think for a mastiff, Clover is perfect, did you want to join us for lunch?" For a person I wanted to keep at a safe distance I found myself trying to stay with her.

"I have a second date, and I was going to join him after helping you. It's going rather well, he's sexy, smooth and a very interesting." Skylar stated.

"Lowering your standards? You used to say adventurous was your type." I didn't see Skylar being a person wanting to stay at home.

"It still is, and he is, at least sexually he's adventurous. I know I haven't been available the way I used to be and I'm sure you wanted to spend more time together before I went back to work, I keep getting the feeling there's something you're not telling me, especially the sudden desire to get a pet." Skylar kept looking me over.

"I know I've watched her for shorter times, but I liked watching Taffy while you were gone, she missed you and I admit I was a bit jealous and thought it would be nice if there was something that missed me that way. It's probably not the best reason to get a pet but at least they will be spoiled." I hadn't wanted to let her know how much I missed her.

"We've always been great friends, shared things with each other even when it was totally inappropriate. How about I come over tomorrow for Taffy and Clover's first playdate?" Skylar was rather excited

"That sounds great." I knew I couldn't get this to last longer.

Skylar leaned in and I don't know if I did it or if she started first, she kissed me on the lips, she might have intended it to be short, but I lingered, the feel of her lips on mine, I kissed her back. Taking a moment before she stepped back.

I hugged Skylar, "thank you for helping me name her, I think your right, I didn't bother eating this morning and I'm sure these two will like getting food soon." I watched Skylar load Taffy in her car, as she waved before leaving.

I kept thinking what an idiot I was. I sat back wondering if I was in my right mind, if it hadn't been for Skylar I wouldn't have done a lot of things I chose to, even though I knew she would disapprove of my meeting the mystery women again. But I kept thinking something like this might be what I need to get Skylar out of my thoughts. Once I was home, it took me a while setting up the animals. Installing a doggy door with a fenced in backyard, that way she could go out any time she wanted, I only hoped the cat didn't have a desire to explore the door. Placing his things on the floor, opening the cage, he stayed inside for quite a while. I wasn't going to force him; he would come out when he felt like it.

I tried to keep busy, and I had to admit I felt guilty not obsessing over Skylar for once. I was looking forward to whoever I was supposed to meet again tonight. I wished they could pick a better location; it wasn't enjoyable climbing down the rocks naked but also walking to my car with nothing to cover with. I was beginning to wonder if my building and adding onto my house was my way of coping with frustration. I built a cute doghouse outside making sure it was fully insulated, not that he would be outside for long but had an option if he wanted to spend time in it. I found myself getting excited that it was starting to get dark outside. I wondered if I had known this person or been with them before, why did I stop seeing them, I don't remember going out with anyone this bold.

I drove my car to the same area as before, this time I left a blanket in my car so I could at least wrap in it when I came back home. I wore nice clothes but nothing I would miss if she decided to cut them up again. Making my way over the rocks and back into the cave, I noticed she had a new piece. There was a soft, thick mat on the floor with a long bench in front of a guillotine, no blade thankfully or I would assume this time it wasn't going to be as fun. There was a note on the bench. It said for me to lay on my stomach with my head through the hole of the guillotine and rest my legs off the sides of the bench, that the magic would do the rest.

For the first time I hesitated before following through. I was curious but had ideas of what was going to happen. I was always open and willing to try pretty much anything at least once before I decided I wasn't going to do it again, I only wished I knew how long the secrecy was going to last before I saw her and what she knew about me.

Hovering over the bench before I first sat down and looked it over more, making sure there wasn't an area that a blade could show up, I rather liked my head and didn't want to lose it. Holding onto the bench, leaning forward with my neck through. Last time everything happened so quickly that I wondered if I was doing this right. It felt like a strange position to be in for her to take advantage of me. Before I had the chance to move, the neck piece dropped locking me in place. A chain cuff from the mattress hooked around my ankle as chains connected to my wrists holding me in place, this time there wasn't a blindfold so I was hoping I would see her for the first time or as she would put it, a second time. That's when I heard her voice.

"I can't help but notice that you seem quite at ease tonight, and I must admit, this evening has very little to do with any plans I had originally thought up—it's more about quenching a peculiar thirst for knowledge that has been stirring within me. To be honest, it may not even fall into the realm of morbid curiosity as much as it leans toward an eccentric fascination of sorts—a quirky little fetish I've acquired over time. So, brace yourself; tonight promises to be an amusing exploration." She started to slide her fingers along my back.

She did exactly what I was expecting, I could feel my clothing getting cut off from me, such a waste of clothing.

"When will you be letting me in on this fetish of yours or even your agenda since I assume you have one now that you've brought it up." I could feel candle wax dripping along my spine.

"Quiet, now is not the time my dear." She stated.

"I would have thought this was the perfect time, I'm still unclear if you are Ella or not." I still tried to figure out who she was.

Not that I would expect this from Ella but if it took tying me up and covering my eyes, maybe it helped her get brave, we broke up amically and was the last person I dated.

"Ella, I must say I love the name, at least you are attempting to do your research. Must you truly disrupt this perfectly good moment by speaking? I was hoping to instead hear a symphony of other delightful sounds emanating from you—perhaps the melodious cries of pain, the dramatic howling reminiscent of a lone wolf under a full moon, or maybe even some heartfelt pleas for more—but not this pesky clarity of thought that you're so insistent on sharing right now!" As she spoke, I could hear other sounds in the background.

There was a larger set of hands now resting on my lower back. It wasn't her and I wondered how many others might be in the room seeing me in this position. I could feel the person rub their hands back and forth giving me a firm massage. I admit it had felt good, but I was mainly waiting to see whatever they were going to do. I could feel something drip over me, not wax this time but a cold oil as the person started to massage it all over my body particularly my buttocks.

Now I knew it wasn't her and I had a feeling what her fetish was as I felt a penis pressing near my backside. Either I had her voice all wrong and she was a man, or she found it to be a turn on watching another man have his way with me, either way I had been willing to accept anything without finding out first.

At least he was being cautious with what he was doing even though I felt like I was being given an enema from the way he squirted a warm oil into my anus. He started to rub himself between my buttocks and not long after started to slowly press against the rim, slowly coaxing himself inside. It was something I had never done before. I had friends who were gay, but none had ever discussed it not that I would have brought it up with them. It was a sensation I wasn't sure how to describe. I liked it but also not at the same time. It was an unusual and perplexing sensation, one that I had never encountered before. While a part of me found it intriguing and enjoyable. My emotional response stirred within me—a blend of appreciation for novelty but also a quiet longing for familiar comfort—left me grappling with my feelings, making the experience all the more fascinating yet unsettling at the same time.

I could feel him sliding in and out of me slowly, each time going in deeper. I was in the perfect position for him to get in his deepest penetration. At least he was slowly warming me up to it. He kept massaging either my back or sides as he kept entering me.

"As I watch you, sprawled effortlessly in that enticing position, surrendering yourself to his every desire, there's an irresistible allure that captivates my senses. The sight stirs a deep craving within me— an overwhelming urge to claim a moment with you for myself, as your beauty exudes an enchanting charm that is hard to resist. How delicious does it feel?"

"Not meaning to ruin the mood, I'm used to things coming out rather than going in. Strangely enough I find it confusing and arousing. Maybe a little faster." I could feel myself slowly getting turned on by the sensations.

Instead of moving slowly he started to thrust much faster as I felt his skin push harder into me, I could feel him slide out almost to the tip of his penis as he would plunge it back in forcing it as far that he could. A few times, he held it in all the way, slightly leaning over me adding more pressure. I felt my legs getting weak, it was a good thing I was on the table. It was rather solid for the amount he was pressing into me and vigorously thrusting. I doubted I was going to have an orgasm, but I hadn't wanted him to stop. It wasn't until he stayed in and started to grind against me that the sensation deepened.

I never in a million years would have tried this if it hadn't been presented to me the way it had and because of it I think the feeling was much better. I could feel him stop for a moment before pulling out. I felt exhausted until I felt a different set of hands on me. A little smaller but hadn't felt like hers.

"Am I going to enjoy you at all tonight?" I was curious how many I would encounter before she touched me again.

"You are at my mercy for at least another four hours. I want you so sore you can barely walk to your car." She gave out a slight evil laugh even though it seemed to turn me on more.

I wished I knew who the five people were that she had penetrated me, some were more careful while a couple were incredibly rough causing me to let out bursts of pain or to use every swear word I knew. She was correct that I wasn't going to be walking after this. Once they were done, I still hadn't seen her walk-in front of me or anyone for that matter. Once they were gone, in the dirt I could see a few footsteps, but nothing to identify anyone. I simply turned over resting until I found I fell asleep. I slept there for a few hours before I was able to leave.

I was thankful this wasn't a popular end of the beach, mainly because of the rocks and lack of sand area. I made my way to my vehicle again, fully naked, walking a little irregularly and thankful to sit down again in my car. Using the blanket, I wrapped myself as I let myself inside my house. feeding the dog and cat, I could see the look on the cat's face as he silently judged me. Closing the door behind me I certainly needed a shower.

# Chapter Four

I was still sore and thankfully only one person noticed, not that I wanted my brother to ask because if he didn't hear what he wanted, he would make sure everyone at the table was asking. I simply said I wasn't used to running with a dog before and that she had a lot of energy, so my legs were tired, at least it was boring enough description for them.

"How is Clover and Otis adjusting?" Skylar asked as Micheal looked confused.

"Skylar helped me pick out a dog and the cat was also from the same home; it didn't feel right separating them. Clover is still shy until I take her for a walk and then she wants to investigate everything. Otis for now judges from a distance, I hope eventually he will let me pet him, he seems to be happy with the little treats I give him."

"Usually, the only commotion is from the jukebox or from dancing. I wonder what's going on back there?" Skylar kept looking back at the bar.

Every so often we could hear the employees raising their voices. I couldn't help but be curious what the staff were arguing about, not something we usually hear at the bar. I made my way up to the counter and could see them in the kitchen with a few different garbage containers. Judy smiled at me as she made her way over to me.

"Did you need something sweety?" She was ready to serve me another drink.

"I was curious what the commotion was. What's up with the trash?" I could see the staff looked confused.

"Someone dumped black dirt or soot into the containers, the large bin outside is filled halfway, at least it doesn't smell bad, it smells like incense." Judy didn't seem too upset by it.

"Do you mind if I take a look at it?" I was curious why someone would dump that much incense in the garbage here at the bar.

She swung the bar door open for me as I walked into the

room. Taking a closer look and smell, I knew it wasn't incense, it was something I had come across before. I didn't want to alarm or upset anyone here, especially their customers.

"Can I talk to you in the corner for a second?" I hoped to keep this quiet.

"Sure," Judy led the way to her office, "I assume you know what it is?" She seemed surprised.

"That's not soot or dirt. You will want to call the police and let them know someone dumped human remains into your bins, that is a lot, and most people don't have that much on hand." Before I could finish speaking, she was on the phone calling the police.

I looked closely at the one bin wondering who or what they were. For the amount it would be a lot of people or depending on the animals, could take up a lot of space. As I made my way back to my group, I noticed she was putting the bins near the back room so no one else would touch them, she looked more worried now not that she shared why. I knew it would be difficult to keep it from everyone once the police car drove up, thankfully they didn't need their lights.

"What did you say to Judy?" Micheal asked me.

"I'll fill you in later. Too many are trying to listen. I barely spent time here while Skylar was gone, did they have a new employee during that time?" I was curious if there was something I missed.

If it made it into the bins outback it could be anyone but if it was inside, it's more likely from an employee or a former employee who had access still. I doubted Judy would change the locks; in a small town it wasn't something most worried about.

"There was a young girl vacationing with her family, she said she was bored so she started working here until they left, they were only staying for the summer, her name was Akuma, she didn't work a lot of hours." Micheal stated with a smile.

"I hope she was legal." Skylar sounded disgusted.

"She was twenty-six, so definitely legal, I'm perverted but not that way. I prefer the older ladies; they know what they want and don't play around. I'm not hunting younger girls; I know what I'm doing and don't need to hide because of lack of experience on my part." Micheal was proud of himself.

"The cabin that normally rents out for the summer near me still has a person living in it, it's a young woman, maybe Akuma stayed longer than the rest of her family." Skylar was now curious.

"We don't know if she's involved, for all we know she could be a sweet and genuinely kind person so I don't want to start accusing her of something, I know I wouldn't like it. This might sound strange, but what did her voice sound like?" I still hoped to find the women from last night.

"Why are you obsessed with people's voices lately? You asked me earlier today." Skylar smiled hoping I would answer her.

"Evidence shows women are drawn to deep male voices." I still didn't want to tell them why.

"But you were asking about a female voice, not a male." Micheal was picking up on the fact I was hiding something.

"I would assume they would agree with me also. I don't want to leave my dog and cat at home for too long alone, they are not used to being alone in the house yet. I'll see you tomorrow, Skylar, enjoy your date tonight." Standing up I hoped to leave before they asked more questions.

I didn't tell them what happened this morning with the cat, I knew Skylar would like to hear it but not exactly Micheal's thing. I had only left for the bathroom this morning and the cat already shredded a few of my pillows. That's okay since they were gifts, and I hated moving them all the time to sit on the couch. I left them there for decoration because Skylar liked it. But the joke was on the cat, I didn't bother picking up the shredded pieces which I think the cat expected. The first thing I did before leaving for the bar this afternoon was to look at the windshield of my car, there was another note. It said, 'three days,' Tucking it in my pocket I didn't want anyone to know I was still getting these.

After being home for a while. I noticed there was something on my kitchen window, opening the door and looking around outside, I hadn't seen anything. Reaching for the note, it said, 'good boy.' I was curious what game she was playing. If it was just a sex game, I could handle that but with other things happening, I did start to worry. Closing the door behind me I heard a sound. I wondered if she came to my door this time when I heard a knock.

I didn't have to wait long, my brother let himself in and sat down on the couch. Otis looked at me before getting on Micheal's lap curling up. It figures he would pick him but that was fine with me. Micheal wasn't thrilled with cats, he preferred dogs. I never had a preference.

"You're my brother so I expect you to be strange but what is up with all the tone of voice crap, what did you say to Judy? You've been distant and for once you're not being moody around Skylar." Micheal was curious showing he wasn't leaving until I told him.

"Something strange is happening in our town, someone knows I was changed but they don't seem to be bribing me other than leaving strange little notes. I don't know if it's tied to what happened at the bar, but someone dumped remains in their bin, a lot of it and the bins inside so I'm guessing it had to be done by an employee or someone who had access to their kitchen. Have you noticed how often Skylar is busy since she got back, for having two weeks off. I thought all of us would be hanging out more. I do wonder if she's dating the same guy or different guys. I know she's outgoing, but this seems strange even for her." I wasn't sure why I blurted all of that out.

"That's more like you, how long have you been holding that in?" Micheal laughed not that he knew all of it.

I felt incredibly nervous but at least he wouldn't guess why. I was curious if the mystery person would have a repeat of last night, I had no idea what to expect anymore. The first night was tame and quick, the second was exhausting and uncomfortable so what was next? Who knows what it would be like or if she would get back to her intent, did she have something to do with the remains and did she intend on doing that to me but because of her fetish or knowing me from before that she's put it off.

"I should have known better than to trust you wouldn't investigate on your own. I did a little checking myself. Akuma has a twin sister. According to a newspaper article from where they said they were from, her sister went missing and had been gone for over a year, the last place she was seen was here. It might explain why they came back here on vacation, possibly hoping to run into her again. The only thing is, when they left, the one sister supposedly stayed behind. I had a friend close by where they live say he saw the one girl with her parents, her name is Akuma and the one staying here says that's her name but it's not, the missing sister waited for them to leave and is acting like she's waiting around trying to find her sister. The other twins' name is Eisheth. Crappy thing to put her parents through. At least they claim they are their parents. I think they are all special creatures of some kind and it's a story they live under to blend in. Other than the two girls being twins, I think they are the only two related. I think we should check out their cabin, it's not far from Skylar." Micheal knew he had my attention once he said Skylar.

Making sure the animals were comfortable, we both got into my car, I was hoping none of the things I was letting the mystery girl do to me would be shared, the last thing I wanted my brother to find out was what happened last night. As we drove past Skylar's house, I noticed she was the only one home. She said she had a date; it could have been cancelled early.

There were no cars parked at the cabin, no lights on or any sign someone had stayed there. Looking in through the windows there wasn't anything personal left out. The doors and windows were locked not that it kept Micheal out very well. Once he picked the door lock, we went in carefully watching where we stepped. I went upstairs while Micheal searched the first floor. There was nothing in any of the cabinets, drawers and the fridge was empty. Upstairs there wasn't any clothing, the bedding had the plastic protective wrap over them for the winter. If the girl said she was staying there, maybe she already left.

"Gregory, you might want to come down and see this." Micheal sounded half worried and a little scared by what he saw.

I came down quickly worried what he found, "what is it?"

Moving the door there was a trash bin in the side room and it was filled with more remains. What worried him was the dead mangled furry body behind the bin. There wasn't a smell coming from it, which was strange, and it was difficult to tell if it was all animal or if there was some human in it, there were parts that could have come from both. Grabbing a broom and giving it a slight push to see the underneath part better, it burst into ashes. There wasn't any blood on the ground.

"At least we know what the ashes are coming from, strange it burst like that." I felt strange as if I was being watched.

"What are you doing in here, she won't like you in her cabin." Skylar started to correct us.

"We were checking it out, besides, we think she left, there's nothing left behind from anyone. If she is staying here, she needs to explain the thing we found that burst into ashes." Micheal was determined to solve this.

"She's not the friendliest person so I suggest we leave so we don't become her next victim. I thought you were not going to check into this, does it have anything to do with the notes that have been left for you?" Skylar wondered as we went out the front door.

"I think it might, but I can't say it definitely is yet." This wasn't something I wanted to explain.

"Have you found anymore notes?" Skylar asked.

"No, I haven't, and I don't expect anymore." We were near the cars, and I hoped to take off before I had to explain more.

"Your lying, you've never been good at it and you're still not. What are you hiding, you went after the person with the notes, haven't you?" Skylar looked at me accusingly.

"I didn't want to admit it but yes and no. I don't know who it is, but I know where they've been meeting me. Unfortunately, I haven't found out anything yet." I didn't know how else to explain it.

"Do they not show up or are there more notes? Why keep showing up if you never see them?" Skylar sounded confused.

"There's something you're not telling us, and I have a feeling its good." Micheal accused.

"There's not much to tell. I found the location, I show up there and the person is there, but I can't see them, they don't say much but what I've found out so far is the person is female and an airy light voice." There was no better way to describe it.

"Why can't you see this person, is it dark?" Skylar was more interested now.

"I would rather not say. We should get going, I want to stop by the bar and see if anyone has been told what the police said about the remains. I'm curious if it's a creature or human." I tried to open my car door, but Micheal slammed it shut.

"Why can't you see the person?" Micheal asked more firmly.

"They use magic to tie me up. Once the blindfold is on, a woman comes into the room, I can hear her footsteps and her voice when she speaks, she told me that she knew me, at some point we dated but I don't remember her voice at all. The main reason she wanted to meet with me is that she had an agenda or purpose not that she's said what that was. She knows something personal about me that I rather not have out." I felt my cheeks flush.

"You slept with her." Micheal laughed.

"How can he sleep with her without seeing her first. I could never have sex with someone I didn't know. But then if I had dated or been with someone before I don't forget them. I've always been incredibly careful, being how everyone expects me to be and I'm tired of it. It's why I've been dating more, why waste my time with one person waiting around to find out if they want more, this way I date more people and have better chances. I want a relationship but even then, I still need to see the person." Skylar tried to make sense of it.

"Maybe he isn't superficial about looks?" Micheal laughed again.

"It has nothing to do with being superficial, I couldn't imagine not knowing what the person I was having sex with looked like. You might be enjoying this but next time it might not go well, it doesn't sound like a safe game to be playing. The next note you get, let us know. I'm going home." Skylar was getting bored of us.

"I think I upset her." I felt worried from the way she took it.

"You're not dating her, you can sleep with other people, it's not as if she isn't, she might not sleep with every guy but she's no virgin. I agree it could get dangerous, maybe the woman is trying to gain your trust before she does something harmful? Call me the next time you get a note from her." Micheal said as he was about to get into his car.

"I already received two more notes from her. There was one on my windshield and the second one I collected off my kitchen window before you got here. One said three nights while the other said good boy. I'm beginning to think she doesn't have anything else in mind other than sex. I don't normally do this kind of thing, but at the moment, I was willing to almost do anything to get Skylar off my mind and it worked temporarily, but I can't ever seem to get away from Skylar." I kept feeling like I should go see Skylar.

"It makes sense, but with the other things, be careful. Next time you get a note, tell me. I'll be at the bar, I'm going to ask a few questions and then see if the station is giving out information or not, depending on how they act, they are either already aware of this or will be surprised by it." Micheal closed his car door and drove off.

I drove over to Skylar's house. She was outside with Taffy throwing a ball to her. Looking up at me, I knew she wasn't expecting me. Getting out of the car, Taffy half jumped up on me to greet me but took off right away to get her favorite ball.

"I'm sorry if I upset you. It was personal and I didn't want to talk about it, but I know I shouldn't have been hiding it." I wanted to apologize but still didn't feel like I was getting it right.

"You're a consenting adult, you don't need my permission. I worry about you and want you to be safe. I've always appreciated how you look after me and I feel like I should be doing more for you. I feel bad we haven't spent much time together but like you, there's things going on in our lives that are personal we don't exactly want to share." Skylar opened the door letting Taffy in.

I followed her into her home. I always felt like everything was in full view with all the open windows, very different from my home. Her home was decorated in beige, light purple and pink tones, a true girly home whereas mine was beige, black and medium blue tones.

"If you ever find yourself in need of anything at all, please don't hesitate to call me. I'm more than willing to help in any way I can, because our friendship has endured for so many years and means the world to me. I told Micheal about a few of the notes I've been receiving, and although it was never my intention to leave you out or make you feel excluded, I've had some concerns about sharing this with either of you because of safety. It's this worry that led me to keep my ongoing experiences private. It's important for me that both of you are safe and protected. I hope we can discuss this openly when the time feels right." I finally felt I explained myself well enough to her.

"Each time you both met, how many times did you have sex?" Skylar was curious.

"We met twice and had sex with each other once." Which was true, I wasn't about to tell her about the other five people I didn't see either.

"Are you meeting her again tonight?" Skylar asked.

"Not for three days, I assume it's at the same place, but Micheal and I were going to try to plan something. I want to find out what she wants." I watched Skylar open a box next to her couch.

Helping her take the plastic off, it looked like an interesting new chair, with only a couple pieces to put together and she pulled a protective cover over it.

"Unusual chair but I like it." As I sat down on it, it tipped forward slightly.

It looked like a half-moon but upside down. It felt incredibly comfortable, and my first thought was it would have been better than the bench I was chained to.

"That's a sex chair, you're not the only one trying something new." Skylar smiled at me knowing I didn't know what I was sitting on.

Jumping up quickly but holding onto Skylar since I felt I was about to knock her over, she laughed slightly as we came closer face to face. I rested my forehead on hers and brushed my nose along hers. I could feel her breath. Sliding my hands from her hips to her lower back. I pulled her closer to me so that I felt her body against mine. Our lips touched not saying a word, I ran my hand halfway down her buttocks gripping them tightly. She kissed me Softley on the lips. I felt intoxicated by her as we kissed. I now ran my right hand up along the inside of her thigh feeling every inch of her. Sliding my hand to the other thigh I massaged her leg going down with a firm grip, then slid back up between her legs. I could feel her breathing deeper as I pulled at her lower lip with my teeth, then going in for a deeper kiss.

"Want to try out the new chair?" Skylar whispered.

"We've been friends for so long, we shouldn't do this. I haven't always been honest with you, there's a reason I don't stay in relationships, and I don't want to ruin this. Micheal and I will be at the bar again tonight, we were going to discuss what we might be able to do with the mystery note person. We could use your opinion." I backed up hoping she wouldn't be too angry with me.

"I'm sure you both will be just fine without me. Whatever you both decide and when, let me know and I'll join you, but for now I have a date to get ready for later tonight." Skylar was happy to be distracted as Taffy tried to take off with one of the couch cushions.

I let myself out, but I still felt I let her down. It felt amazing to be that close to her. I wished I could do more but if this person was blackmailing me, she could get hurt. I'm a monster, I have no idea what I was turned into, and it might not seem like a big deal since my brother knows and I've been intimate with others but one of my premonitions I had years ago still hadn't changed, I might have stopped it, but I don't need to help it. I kept seeing her lying on the ground dead, bleeding and I hoped whatever mystery was going on in town wasn't how that happened to her. It's also why I worried she was dating more than she used to. When she told me she had secrets she hadn't told me, I was curious what they were. She had always told me everything even though I assumed she had, but then I wasn't much better.

# Chapter Five

I hadn't seen Skylar for the last two days. Not that Micheal and I knew what we were going to do. If we both showed up, one of us would be locked up and who knows what they would do with the other unless I could hide Micheal. Even though I'm positive he doesn't want to see me naked which seems to happen every time. When we were at the diner, no one was talking about the remains and Judy took time off for a few weeks. No one was being reported missing, everyone was walking around and living as if nothing was wrong. Then I heard a disgusted sound from the kitchen. Looking back there was a couple of employees looking into one of their bins, it was filled with remains again. I watched as they brought it out back. Micheal was already planning the same thing. He went and started to joke and keep the staff busy while I went outside and to the back of the building. Pulling a bag out of my pocket, I shook the bin a little as the remains separated from other trash and slowly slid into the bag. Looking at it I wondered, who are you? Slipping it back into my pocket and waving to Micheal, I got in my car and drove straight to his house.

Micheal wasn't far behind as we went into his home. Micheal wanted to be a forensic scientist when he was younger except for many reasons was either discouraged or turned away that he eventually gave up. However, he had invested in a lot of money into the equipment and was still using it.

Normally there wouldn't be any DNA left in the ashes, what he hoped to find was anything else in it that might remain. Using a special sifter held over a glass plate, he poured the ash into the sifter and tapped the side until most had gone through. There were several tiny splinters or small pieces.

"Hopefully these are teeth, and we can test it." Micheal sounded confidant.

"How long do you think it will take." I leaned over his

shoulder to watch.

"Do you mind? Give me a little space, go home and play with your fur things and I'll call you when I find out. I do better when you're not watching over my shoulder." Micheal was getting frustrated.

"Fine, but your being mean." I couldn't help it, I used to accuse my brother of being mean when we were kids.

Not that I knew what else to do, I made my way home, sort of, I made a slight detour. I drove past Skylar's home when I noticed only her car was there. Driving slightly past, I parked down the street a short distance from Skylar. I kept wanting to see her after the way I left things.

I walked up to the door to find it open a smidge, which I thought was strange for her. Walking in, all I could see was a long line of tea light candles lighting the way. Taffy had been left in the guest room while Skylar was in her bedroom. The room was illuminated with candles.

She looked incredibly enticing there, tied to the bed. I wished I could have done this with her, but I doubted she saw me this way, I was the safe trusting friend. If she only knew the thoughts that went through my mind. I don't know how he managed to get girls to do this for him, he could do anything but the most I would get is coffee out but then I also held back too much. She would never know I was here, the silk blindfold over her eyes, hands handcuffed to a different corner of the bed. Her legs were bound to the footposts. She simply lay there waiting for him to seduce her.

I stood at the foot of her bed admiring her body, the heat that I could feel coming from her, the vanilla scent she always wore. I started to think I was crazy for not only watching her have sex with another man but to be in her bedroom when she wasn't expecting me during an intimate moment. But my brain wasn't exactly cooperating with me. I dropped my slacks to the ground, arguing with myself the whole time telling myself not to, but I kept moving anyway. Kneeling on the bed, the weight shifted, and she knew someone was there. Moving between her legs sliding my hands up along her sides, I loved the way she felt.

Leaning over her nuzzling her pussy with my nose, she tried to shift a little as I placed my hands on her hips holding her still. Licking her, I knew I was obsessed with her when my first thought was how great she tasted, dipping my tongue in deeper as she let out a moan. Wiggling my tongue in her and then I started to suck on her which she seemed to like. I enjoyed feeling her trying to move as I now sat up, moving her legs so they would be over mine slightly, she had a little space to move but not once I was under her. Kneeling I was in the best position, placing my penis over her labia, I rubbed her with it. Pressing it at the opening of her vagina and now putting my hands on her hips. Sliding into her, I rhythmically slid in and out. Occasionally I pressed trying to get in as far as I could. Now thrusting quickly and leaning over her slightly pulling upward.

There were so many other positions I wished I could get her into. Pulling out of her and moving to the side, I sat next to her, placing my fingers near her pussy playing with it. Sticking a finger in and wiggling it around and adding another finger, I kept adding until I had all four. I started to thrust my fingers back and forth as I would have with my penis. This way I could go much faster. As I did, I could feel her raise her hips upward and moaning much louder. I did this for a while until I could feel her orgasm. Taking my fingers out, I back up off the bed. I couldn't help it but if I had her waiting for me like this, I wouldn't bother going to work, I would spend the entire day pleasuring her. Putting my clothes back on and not saying a word the entire time, I walked out of the house and down the road. I was a short distance from the house when I saw him drive by, he waved to me, and I smiled waving back. Not for the same reason but I knew I warmed her up for him.

Once I made it home, I looked at my phone to see Micheal left a message. I played the recording, Micheal said the result would surprise me, it was more animal with the smallest hint of human. So, we were dealing with a special creature unless they were not careful and mixed the ashes from both.

There were two more calls, one where Micheal stated he talked to a friend about rumors or rituals in the forest not far from the caves. Then the third call from him was telling me to get down to the caves, it might not have been a third night yet, but I needed to see what was going on. Making sure the animals were secure and locking the windows and doors behind me. For some reason I was feeling paranoid for the first time. I rarely needed to lock my doors out here.

Driving my car down the usual path until I had seen my brother's truck parked on the side of the road before the road splits into three directions. I parked next to him and walked the rest of the way. Coming close to the cave, I could see my brother looking from up top. Instead of going in front of the caves, I made my way through the thick trees and vines that were crowding the area, stumbling a few times on a few rocks and fallen trees, I made it up next to him. We were able to look over from the top of the hill and looking down there were people coming in and out of the caves. Then we saw the twin sisters, both were there. Most of the girls were wearing see through lace dresses while the men wore simple briefs. They were wading in the water watching as if waiting for something.

"How long has this been going on?" I was curious when something would happen.

"I think they were waiting for others to join them. None are coming from the direction we did, they all come walking along the water to the left beach side. Once we get here it's like they have it memorized where to stand, and they wait and look out over the water." Micheal kept watching.

It wasn't until there was a large group, roughly thirty people, that bubbles started to form. The twins were standing out front as the water started to churn up even more. I kept trying to see if I recognized any of them, but I hadn't until the one girl spoke. I knew that voice, it was a voice you didn't forget so how could I if we had dated or even been together before? Was she messing with me?

They started to chant something low enough that we couldn't hear but it sounded vibrational. They tossed something in the water, but we were not close enough to see what it was. It was the strangest site to watch. Lumps of water would draw upward and form looking like a human until they walked past the group. The further they went, the more human of an appearance they had. They took on the appearance of those in the water, as each one replicated someone, that person would follow them into the cave.

Once they were all in, we made our way down and around to the side. We were hoping to see what they were doing with these creatures, unsure if they created them or if they were already in the water, possibly alien from another world or simply the water where mankind has never been able to get to. Not that the water here was very deep. But how did they find them? The closer we came to the rim of the cave, there were little sparks of white shooting out from the cave, curious, we tried to see except they had the opening closed off.

Mutually we decided to walk back to the vehicles. On our way there Micheal kept looking at me and I wondered what he was thinking.

"Why do you keep looking at me?" Whatever he was thinking, I wanted him to get it out.

"You're not normally the impulsive type, you stay to yourself, I can keep track of all the girls you dated on one hand. You became rather bold, if this whole operation wasn't involved in something that could get you killed, I would encourage you to stick with it. I feel strange for saying that, but it was nice having you more determined. I think Skylar picked up on it and liked it." Micheal stopped once we were near his truck.

"Seeing what they were doing down there and knowing I was tied up in there, kind of scares me how stupid I was but I admit, I was getting into it. Kind of like a kinky pre-party but I don't want to be part of what's going down there now. Not that I fully understand that, and we watched it, I wish she would let me ask her questions." I felt more confused than before.

When I looked at my vehicle, there was another note. Maybe it wasn't her? Could it possibly be someone else, at least it would make sense since I didn't recognize anyone, and she said we had been together. Micheal watched as I took the note off, this time it was longer than the usual few words.

"You're both invited to a discovery party, there will be clues explicit for each person, if you find another person's clue, it is not for you. Each card will have a color, once the color is assigned, those are the only notes you are to follow, each is numbered so you will know if you missed any or how much further you have. Only a few at the end will have questions answered, others will feel triumphant pain, some pleasure, while others will enjoy a party of a lifetime. Begin your day in your best attire, there will be an outfit for you to wear hanging in your closet at home. You are to bring Skylar and your brother Micheal. The event begins in the morning, each will find a note on their front door."

As I read this to Micheal, we both wondered if it was worth investigating or possibly it was time to include authorities, not that we could claim anyone had been harmed or about to other then the strange scene we watched at the beach.

"I understand neither of us are home, but I doubt Clover or Taffy will let anyone in the houses to leave clothing. I'll call you when I get home when I find out what they've done if they were able to get in." I was worried since Skylar was home, if they would do anything to her.

Before going home, I drove past Skylar's home. There was still the car from her date there, I was curious if her date was part of this thing or if he was innocent, nothing looked out of order as I saw the door open letting Taffy back in. Going home I wanted to see if they were able to or would risk trying to get into my place. As I drove down my road, there was another car leaving, the person was covering their face making me curious if they were hiding themselves or simply resting their hand over their face from boredom.

Pulling up the drive it looked perfectly normal, nothing out of the ordinary except for the new nail next to my door. There was a hanger with a clothing bag hanging from it. I know I read it would be inside my house in my closet, but I was betting Clover never let them in. Opening the door, I could saw Clover sound asleep on the couch while the Otis was in the middle of the entry way with blood down the side of his face and a piece of fabric still in his mouth. He was glaring at me as if I didn't get his permission first before letting someone else inside. It wasn't something I would have guessed but it looked like the cat kept them from entering, he seemed rather proud of himself as he dropped the fabric piece on the floor in front of me and then slowly walked away. Giving the dog a slap, the cat took over the couch while Clover gave up and laid down on the floor.

I took the bag and carried it back to my bedroom, closed the door since I didn't want to risk the cat touching it. Hanging it up on the back of the door and unzipping it, I wasn't sure what to expect. Pulling it out I was impressed; it was certainly fancy, but I was curious how the game was going to be run. Especially if everyone was dressed up. At the bottom there was a card with the address and a map of where to meet. It wasn't at the cave again which was good if we had to wear the new shoes they provided, and if the women wore heals, those were not getting over the rocks.

There was a three piece double breasted black suit with oxford dress shoes. I would have preferred my own shoes, but I assumed they wanted these for a reason. I could hear scratching at my door, so I put the suit back in the bag to protect it. Opening the door the cat came in meowing at me sounding upset as he hissed a few times. Picking him up and placing him in the window, he looked at me strangely before lying flat enjoying the remainder of sunshine. I swear the sun is the cat's Achilles heel.

"If you turn into a person and were a special creature, similar to werewolves, I'm going to be mad at you, I've been naked in front of you." Giving me a one-eyed blink, I went back into the living room, I felt safer with the dog.

# Chapter Six

We chose to come together in Skylar's car. She was surprised to see the note on her door. When her date left, he pulled it off and handed it to her, waiting to see if she needed him. Letting him know it was alright, most likely from a friend, she kept it closed, said goodbye to him and went back inside. She checked her bedroom since she was spending the time in the living room. Taffy hadn't come rushing out as she usually would have. Instead, she was still lying in the middle of the room slowly eating a steak that was left for her on a plate. Inside her closet was a dress, shoes, and jewelry. Her note was identical to ours.

I would find this to be an interesting adventure except if it included my brother and best friend, now I would worry if there was an ulterior motive behind all of this. When we arrived, there was a person parking the cars. We all got out as they drove the car over to the parking lot. It looked like a beautiful traditional banquet hall building from the outside with several little windows, a few trellises in various places with white benches underneath. Now having the front doors opened, we entered taking in a breath and being amazed at the scene. There were jade marble furniture and an impressive staircase at the end of the room.

Couples were sitting around the room either talking or to the side, a few were dancing with each other to the classical music that was playing. Desert trays were on the left side with a few people over there. There were a few others from town we recognized and talked to for a while before the party started. Apparently, this wasn't the first time the mystery lady threw one of these and the other guests were talking about some of the prizes that were given out at the end. Hearing it has happened before put us at ease a little bit.

A lady in a lace dress was handing out envelopes to each person. As she handed us ours, we pulled out the card, neither of us had a color close to the other. Mine was blue, Skylar had purple and Micheal had orange. Both Micheal and Skylar had the number four in the corner of their card while mine showed five. Each came with their own clues. My first one started with, "it is found under something soft." Other than that, there wasn't much of a hint.

We waited, hoping there might be a starting time for this since it seemed strange, we might be looking in this room with everyone else. The building from the outside was rather large but it was going to be interesting, I hoped it was simply a harmless game. I didn't like the idea of separating from the others.

Soon the music stopped while a gentleman stood on the end of the staircase, he announced we would be starting in a few seconds. Moving off from the stairs, he stepped to the side as the set of stairs rose into the air showing a hidden room down below with several stairs going down. Small lights started brightening the room as everyone went down following the host. There was an incredibly long hallway with several doors off to either side.

"As you will learn there is quite a large labyrinth below the mansion. Follow your clues and you will end up with your personal prize at the end of it. I wish all of you good luck and hope if you enjoy this you will join us again." Stepping aside, several were ready to start.

"At least if they want us to enjoy this and come again, I think we can scratch potential death off the list." Micheal sounded relieved.

"Keep these on you, that way if you don't end up outside or wherever we are supposed to go after this is over, we can find you. I would rather be careful then wish we had these." Skylar handed each of us a small clip to put on our shoes.

We followed everyone down the stairs. I watched as Micheal and Skylar went into the same room with several others, there were a few who had gone into the same room as I did. So far, I didn't recognize anyone and none of them were from town. I wished Skylar could have come with me. Everyone looked confused as we looked around the room. It looked like a typical bedroom. Nothing out of the ordinary. I searched around pillows. I found a yellow card, but I was supposed to stick with my color. A lady pulled the card from my hand excited that I found it for her. She read her card, and her question was rather simple, it told her to look in the closet. Opening it up, she walked in and closed the door behind her. I watched as another person pulled at a corner of a painting, at first it didn't do anything, then they pulled at the other side, and it swung open. Stepping in, they disappeared. I was the last one remaining in the room. I searched everywhere until I lifted the soft area rug on the side of the bed. There was a blue card there. It read, "go into the closet, follow the path ahead until you see your card on one of the doors.

Opening the closet, I stepped in and followed the instructions. There were eight doors until I came to the one with my card on it. Opening it I was hoping it was going to be more than going from room to room or this wasn't going to last long. Reading the note it stated, "everyone receives first and gives second. Open the door with the number seven, no lights and find something comfortable to lie down on. "

It was a good thing I had already been introduced to this before because I was positive it was going to be the same thing again; except I wasn't sure if I was going to enjoy it or get turned on because she wasn't watching. There weren't exactly no lights, there was the slightest glow thankfully or I would have stumbled over things. One wall resembled a two-way mirror, I was curious who might be on the other side watching. I can't say the furniture in here was anywhere resembling normal. One felt like it had table stand legs supporting a large round circle, not flat but upward with a hole in the middle. How was I supposed to sit on that unless they meant for me to be inside it. There was another like it except it was in a large u-shape except upside down. There was a mattress on the floor in the far corner, not that it was comfortable. I wasn't sure what they wanted since no one else seemed to be in the room with me.

Maybe they would get the hint of what I was in the mood for if I laid on my back. Stretching out on the floor pad, there was a soft cloth covering it but not much to it. I wasn't adventures to try out the others. I waited until I felt the familiar feeling of straps around my wrists and ankles. But then someone was now standing next to me, pushing a thick pillow under my lower back raising me up. I wondered if they did this with everyone or just me. Maybe because I didn't brag about having sex with women, did they think I was gay? I doubted they could do much with me if they didn't want to ruin such nice clothing. I thought this too soon. I felt the same feeling of scissors cutting away my clothing, I certainly hoped they had something for us to change into. Skylar was not going to appreciate them destroying her dress, she had told us how much she loved it. But then the idea of someone else having her in the dark, tying her up making out with her anyway they wished made me incredibly jealous. The feel of her body was amazing. I was deep in thought thinking of Skylar when I should have been paying attention to the one standing over me, placing my penis into, he slowly slid down. I was confused because I thought I might be the one doing it this time. It did say, "receives first and gives second."

He kept sliding up and down when I felt a second set of hands on me. Kneeling on the ground, he went a little faster entering which caused a pinch that hurt. I was slightly tighter this time not that the person seemed to care, pushing against the pressure, he didn't use much lube as he thrust back and forth. Both became rhythmic with each other, it felt strange lying there not being able to do anything. The one held onto my buttocks tightly, using it to help him thrust more deeply. The gentleman on top started to grind, keeping low on me.

I noticed the two-way mirror started to shimmer slightly and I wondered why it was doing that. The dark part of the mirror now revealed who was on the other side, it was another room like this. Lying on the edge of a flat table on their stomach with their hands behind their back holding onto their ankles with legs spread slightly. There was a man standing behind her entering her. I could see her watching me. As I was thrust into, she licked her lips and gave me a one-eyed blink. I was positive she was feeling turned on from watching me get pounded in the ass. Even though I felt jealous before thinking of someone else enjoying her, it was a turn on watching him thrust into her as she watched me. The man thrusting into me, kept pushing harder against me, now pressing his thumb in slightly with his penis making it tighter.

I watched as the person with Skylar dripped oil over her anus, as he slid from her vagina up and over to the rim and slowly pushed in. She reacted more the deeper he went in. Once all the way in, he slightly arched over her adding a little pressure as he continued to thrust back and forth getting into a rhythmic sync also. I felt incredibly turned on watching her body move as he pushed into her.

What I didn't like was when the mirror started to darken again, and she disappeared. I didn't know if they simply started or were ending. I wanted to continue watching her, but the mirror didn't clear up again.

I hadn't orgasmed the last time, but I could feel an intense rush come over me, I was already in the mood when the evening started when I saw how Skylar's backside looked in the dress, it clung to her curves perfectly. After I climaxed, I was sore, but they kept going until I heard a light ding. Both pulled off and moved away from me, leaving me there naked. The restraints unhooked by themselves again and the other two people were already gone from the room.

It took me a few minutes to get up. I felt along the wall for the light. Turning it on, I could see a card on the back of the door. Taking it off and reading it the card read, "have you ever been caught in action? Go out the opposite door you came in until you find the next blue card."

It felt strange to get a card but no action with it, not that I minded after this last one. I already felt this one happened with Skylar watching me get screwed by two men. Opening the other door and leaving through it, I still hadn't seen anyone through the hallway. I was already beginning to get lost even though I was positive I could still find my way out. Maybe it was a good thing Skylar gave us these trackers to put on our shoes.

It felt strange walking around with shoes on and naked. I wasn't sure when we would run into each other, if we're ever meant to mingle, which is why I wondered how they could have so many people participating in this and not run into any of them. There could have been an unground city here with the way the tunnels were. Walking down a short distance I hoped I might run into Skylar. I was curious how my brother was doing but mentally begging not to run into him until we left. Soon I saw another blue card on the door. pulling it off and taking it out of the envelope, I took a deep breath and hoped it was going to get better. At least now I expected the whole thing to be a sex party. The card was rather simple. It said, "everyone must eat at some point."

I was starting to wonder if we would be eating something off others, others doing that to us or would we physically sit down and eat something. Opening the door, it led into a large open room. There were already several people in here, thankfully all were naked even though I still felt self-conscious. I would never intentionally walk around nude in front of so many strangers, I wasn't the type even to go to a nudist beach. There was a buffet and several tables with odd looking chairs. Places were assigned so I couldn't sit with Skylar or my brother even though it felt strange being around so many people while being naked.

Grabbing a plate and sitting down with it, I put the card that was on the table with my stack I was carrying with me. It felt strange sitting next to the others. They were busy talking, all I had to do was listen.

"What did you think of the water. Wasn't that creepy having it look exactly like you?" The woman to the left of me asked.

"Mine didn't last long. She said something about not having enough energy. After lunch I'll be collecting my prize before I leave for home." The gentleman on the right of me said.

"Same as myself. I don't get any more cards after this; the group has been cut in half. I am curious what they are using to decide who leaves early or not. The names are up on the board." The lady in front of me stated.

"If my name is on the board, is there a card over there?" I was curious where to get the next one since the only person working was handing out plates.

"It's on the bottom of your plate." The woman on the right of me said.

Lifting my plate slightly, I felt under my plate and realized there was a card still. Pulling it out and being careful not to share where I was going next, the card read, "when you're done eating, it's time to relax and soak."

"I think I get to experience the water now. Hopefully it's fun." Getting up from the table I walked towards Micheal and Skylar.

"Did either of you get a card again?" I was curious who would be stuck staying longer.

"I didn't and I'm not on the board. Supposedly the prizes are in the main ballroom where we were before. There's a room to the side here that has clothes, and I can't wait to get dressed. I don't have issues with my body, but I'm not used to being around this many people while being naked. I had no idea it was going to be a nudist party." Micheal kept looking around to see who watching him.

"I have another card also saying the same thing. Half the people at our table have already been to the next part. If you look at the board, there are only seven people left. They said it was cut in half but that's more than half, I would have guessed three to four hundred people came today. I am curious why they picked us to keep going. I'm hoping we get another two-way mirror, that was a rather sexy view, I know it's something I've dreamed of." Skylar smiled at me.

"What two-way mirror?" Micheal tried hiding his smile realizing we were hiding something.

"I'm not sharing that. Quick question, do people think I'm gay?" I wasn't sure how they were going to answer.

"We met when we were kids, I wasn't thinking about anything like that until we were in our teens. I had several friends think you were cute, but they always ended their comments by, 'to bad he's gay." Skylar laughed.

"Did you ever correct them?" I looked between her and my brother.

"I encouraged it. I was popular because I knew the right words to charm a girl, but they were your friend since they thought you were, that friend." Micheal laughed also.

"Besides, the right person thought you were cute, and you never noticed her. Have fun with the rest of this thing." Skylar smiled as she walked away from us.

"You do realize she's talking about her." Micheal stated.

"If she's with me, she'll end up dead. They all do. I dated the one girl regardless of the vision and where did that get us? She died exactly the way I saw it." My vision kept changing but the end stayed the same.

"That wasn't exactly a safe corner, unfortunately a lot of drivers have died there because of poor visibility. She's already with you, the line was crossed a long time ago and not that long ago, you obliterated that thing. I'll be waiting for you both in the main lobby." Micheal stated as he turned to leave.

If I hadn't been here, I simply would have been playing with my new furry family members. Skylar would be safe; I would get together with Micheal when he was in the mood to investigate things. I know it helps to get right in the middle of the storm to find out what is going on. I hoped they might view me as anyone else. I wanted to find out what they were doing with these water people and why there were so many ashes being produced. I simply hoped it would turn out to be nothing but an illusion. As much as I was attracted to Skylar. Micheal was right, I have crossed the line many times but how do I explain to her I keep seeing her dying in front of me. Taking a deep breath, I followed down the hallway, through a door and looked again for my number. The sex part of the party was starting to lose its appeal.

# Chapter Seven

Before opening the next door, I hesitated for a few seconds, took a deep breath and then opened it. I was certainly impressed with the look of the room. There was creeping ivy everywhere, pretty flowers, a floor that looked like rock but was soft and spongy, a hot tub in the center of the room with a small grotto on the other side next to the wet sauna. Closing the door behind me I walked over to the sauna, still looking around but no one was there, I was the only one in the room. This would be nice if all I had to deal with was the sauna. I felt strange the only thing they left had been the shoes. I left those outside of the sauna, I didn't want to risk getting the tracker wet. Opening the glass door to it, I went in half expecting to see someone in there but thankfully I was still alone. The seating inside was extremely comfortable as I sat down, leaning against the wall feeling the warm steam and dripping water around me. I was incredibly relaxed enough I managed to take a ten-minute nap.

As I stepped out of the sauna, I still expected to see someone except I still hadn't. There wasn't anyone else in the room, no two-way mirror or anything that looked like a card telling me to leave yet. I hadn't bothered to put the shoes back on, but I did take the tracker off, lifted a chunk of my hair and clipped it to my hair so that I could hide it and hopefully keep it out of the water. Slowly walking over to the hot tub, I kept waiting for someone to come in, but they hadn't.

As I gently stepped down into the inviting warmth of the hot tub, a wave of soothing relief washed over my weary muscles, enveloping me in warmth that felt like a cozy blanket hugging my sore muscles. The moment I laid back and surrendered to the soothing jets of water caressing my body. With each passing moment, I found myself drifting deeper into blissful serenity, secretly hoping that this was to be my final room assignment, all my worries melted away; it was as if each bubble whispered sweet nothings to my sore back and legs.

I hadn't been in very many rooms, so I was curious if everyone experienced the same things or if there were different options offered. While relaxing and sitting in the hot tub, allowing myself to unwind as the invigorating jets came to life by being stronger, soothing my muscles and calming my mind. However, amidst this tranquil moment, an unsettling development occurred; I noticed that the water turned a light blue and beside me something physical began to take shape, eventually forming a figure that mirrored my own likeness with uncanny precision. As I turned to look at this unexpected doppelgänger, a sense of unease washed over me—was it merely a figment of my imagination, was the heat getting to me or what the others explained of their experience. It hadn't looked at me once and I wasn't sure if I should speak to it.

"How long have you been in the water, should I get out? I don't want to be soaking if I'm inside of someone." It creeped me out knowing the water surrounding me could be a person.

The water creature gurgled slightly, before saying, "We'll move over here," standing up, the rest of the water formed into identical forms of myself stepping out of the hot tub. There wasn't a drop of water left.

I got out of the tub quickly feeling grossed out by what happened. The door on the other side of the room opened with both Akuma and Eisheth coming through the door, both took a few minutes looking over the water creatures.

"I'm confused by all of this, you both looked shocked by this, but I assume from the others talking about it, you already know about this." As I pointed at the creatures.

"These are the best specimens; they've never spoken before. We'll see how long these last and if it goes well, we will finally move forward with our goals, and you will have so much admiration." Eisheth seemed impressed as she looked the creatures over.

"Why would I get admiration? What are these things and why do they look like me? What goal are you working on?" I doubted they would answer my questions, but it was difficult to hold the most basic ones back.

"You are so cute; you deserve admiration for participating and helping us accomplish such great goals. We found without clothing, it's easier to get the water to naturally form into its surroundings. Eventually people won't know if it's the real thing or a substitute. We have your last room ready for you and then you can collect your gift." Akuma smiled as she handed some clothing to me.

"Why does it have to look like me?" I hadn't hesitated to get dressed.

"Can you think of better-looking people? Perhaps the ones you were intimate with, not that they are around any longer, they were temporary water creatures." Akuma sounded proud of their creatures.

"Do they think and feel?" I could have sworn I was with a real person.

"They don't have brains, similar to the concept of an egregore but instead of clay they are made from water and other ingredients. Imagine all the possibilities and they won't be robotic, no one will be able to tell if they are truly real or simply a sex doll. By watching you have sex with them, we get to see your genuine response to them. Now that your time is done in here, please move into the next room." Akuma and Eisheth stood on either side of me, ushering me out of the room.

That felt strange, how many people that were here were not the real people and did they do anything with the real ones? The people around me felt far too real even though I did wonder why they hadn't spoken, the only ones who talked were at lunch not that I was around to many. Now I was worried about Skylar and if they would make a replica of her. I still hadn't learned where the ash was coming from, but now they are trying to replace people but for what reason unless it was for sex games. Mentally I was confused how to feel about this. Sex dolls have been around for an extremely long time, and they've improved them to the point of looking realistic, but this, they felt realistic but are from water. What makes them move on their own?

The hallway started to lead upward until I came to a wall with a strange door. Not sure what was going to happen next, I opened the door and walked in. It looked like a regular living room, fireplace, couch and a couple comfortable chairs. Skylar was sitting on the couch until she saw me and stood up looking incredibly nervous.

"Are you actually Gregory or a water thing?" She kept trying to look me over.

"I'm the real person, I've noticed the fakes don't show expression or any natural sound, when they do its still off a little. I thought we would be solving a massive crime but so far, I'm not finding anything unless there's more to these water creatures. Anything can be used for evil intentions but that's the whole thing, what is their intentions for this?" I went and sat down on the couch.

"I don't like the possibility of them making a replica of me without my permission and someone having sex with it. There were so many attractive people but so far, it's just us unless they've already done this before. There's so much they are not telling us." Skylar kept looking around the room.

The room started to shake as we pulled strongly in one direction. We started to hear metal clinking sounds as both doors locked shut and the walls wobbled slightly. From the way the room was moving we doubted it was stationary any longer. There wasn't anywhere to look out, I did manage to pry the door open but there were bars on the other side. We were traveling down a worn-out road with grass growing through showing it wasn't used anymore. I wished I had my cell phone but that and my wallet were left back in my clothes that were originally cut off from me. I was thankful to have the tracker in my hair so maybe Micheal could find where we were and then a moment of panic, did they let him leave? They knew he was my brother so how would they explain to him where we were since we were not joining him. The sun started to rise, and I worried if this was where I lost Skylar.

"Do you recognize where we are?" Skylar asked.

"I've never seen this area, I know I haven't covered our entire county, but this doesn't look like anything around us, at least the pathway doesn't give away much. I don't think we have much choice but to wait and see what they have planned and where they are taking us. Either way from this point on, I don't think it's safe if we are asked to separate from each other, they need to tell us what they are doing, so from now on we stick together." I hoped Skylar hadn't felt I was forcing her.

"I agree, I think we are safer together." Thankfully Skylar hadn't hesitated to agree with me.

Leaving the door open so we could at least see the outside, we sat next to each other on the couch enduring the shaking and rumbling of the box we were locked in wondering how much longer we were going to be in here. Both of us were tired but neither wanted to risk being pulled apart if we did fall asleep. I had Skylar rest first while I kept watch, after she woke, I slept a little not that it was easy with the way the couch wobbled and shook. After a while I didn't need Skylar to wake me as we jerked to a quick stop. The outside was already dark out when a person came to the back and stopped right in front of the door.

"Are you going to tell us where we are at?" Skylar asked the person.

They never once looked up or reached for the door, they had no reaction other than to burst into dust. A second person came back who at least showed some expression while opening the door letting us out. Not that we knew where here was. They had to place steps in front of the door so we could step down. As we had I assisted Skylar safely down.

"Follow the pathway to your next area. If you go over the side, the bushes are covering the fact we are surrounded by a steep cliff, so I don't recommend trying to take off." He simply stood there waiting for us to pass him.

I held Skylar's hand as I looked over the side, the building we were in and driven here blocked the only bridge coming over to the center island, we were not only on a high-end Cliff but there was water several feet down in the color of orange. I wasn't sure if I wanted to risk swimming in it. Following the path forward, there was a stone building in front with another person with no expression standing next to it. The door was already open as we walked in, the creature pushed the button and turned towards us before bursting into ashes.

"I'm guessing these creatures don't last long unless they don't do well when they are outside?" I was curious why they kept bursting in front of us.

"I think they are looking for a way to make them last longer by using us somehow." Skylar looked around the elevator.

"What could we possibly do, neither of us are scientists, at least you're in the medical field but I doubt you could make these things last longer.

"I was heavily involved in witchcraft in my teens but what we did isn't anything that can help them. I did get extremely good at various fields of it, but I doubt they know. I have a feeling if we get stuck down there, we will never get out. I've held back secrets from you and I'm pretty sure they figured it out, we need to find a way out of this elevator." Skylar started to look around for a way out. Detaching the top, she dropped the panel down.

Pushing the black button prevented the elevator from going any further down. Using my hands to hoist her up at first, she was able to get the emergency latch to drop from the ceiling. Skylar jumped slightly grabbing the rim of the opening and pulled herself out, she knew I wasn't going to stay behind. I grabbed the sides and hoisted myself out following behind her. There was a rail she started to climb upward. She made her way out and waited for me to join her. Looking around, there hadn't been anyone outside. I doubted anyone expected us to try and get out. Looking around the edges, there were only steep cliffs until Skylar suggested a particular side down. At least the times my premonitions showed her dying, it was always inside a building.

"The vines are strong enough here, we can use them to climb down. I haven't figured out how to cross the orange water yet, I'm hoping its rust and not something toxic." She said as she already started climbing down.

"At least wait for me." I tried to keep up with her, I had never seen her like this before.

"What secret are you keeping that they would want you for?" I felt confused.

"I would rather not say if I don't have to but I'm sure I'll have to explain soon." She kept climbing down until she reached the lowest point before the water.

Grabbing a leaf, she dropped it into the water and watched it float, waiting to see if it would copy the leaf or disintegrate it. So far nothing happened to it, she was about to dip her finger in the water to test it when I stopped her.

"If either of us are going to get disfigured I would rather, have it be me then you." Before she could respond I put my hand in the water and an electric shock ran through the water not that I felt any pain when I pulled my hand back.

"Jump in and swim across the water before it disappears, or we will be stuck on this side." Skylar stated as she jumped in.

Skylar trusted that I wouldn't hang back questioning her logic, instead I followed behind and swam quickly not that I was a fast swimmer like her. We barely made it to the other side as the water was lowering and instead of being replaced by actual water, the water creatures were multiplying looking like our identical duplicates filling the pit. Pulling myself out, I looked back to see that all the water was gone and where the water was, it was filled with duplicates of us. They all stood there not moving.

Looking back, Skylar was already climbing up the other side of the hill, I must admit when she's determined she can accomplish anything. Following behind and I stress following, I was having a difficult time keeping up with her. We made it up to the top and through the thick forest, I wasn't sure if she knew where she was going but at least it was in the opposite direction of the place we were getting away from. I was never good with direction. I could stand in the middle of a forest and end up going in circles not knowing it. Skylar was more of a natural and never lost her sense of direction.

When we got to a slight clearing Skylar started to run and yelled back to me, "try to keep up best you can." Not that I was taking my time, but I had never seen her run this fast before. I might have been healthy, but running was never my thing, truthfully, I hated running. We cleared the open area and back under the dense trees again which is when she started to slow down. I guessed she was worried we would be easily seen from overhead if we stayed in the clearing too long. We could no longer see the area we ran from. Coming to a rather large tree, Skylar stopped and leaned against it waiting for me to catch up. As I had I dropped to the ground to take a deep breath and hoped we were not going to run anymore or at least could take a break. I doubted they would have assumed we went this way or this far

# Chapter Eight

"We can't stay here, eventually they will find out we escaped." Skylar kept looking back for any movement.

"I doubt they will be sending those water creatures after us, I don't think they are capable of doing much." I started to walk alongside Skylar keeping pace.

"Why do you think they want you? I highly doubt any secret you've kept would keep a group like this after you let alone trying to involve all of us." Not that I wanted to share mine.

"Did you ever wonder what happened to my parents. The fact my grandparents raised me, I never could tell anyone because I didn't know who I could trust. They were killed and the order didn't know I was aware of it. They simply think I believe they died in a car crash. I found out from a former member who told me I would need to protect myself from them some day." She looked worried about how I would take it.

"It could have been someone messing with you. People can be evil when they want to hurt someone." I didn't feel I was being fair when I had my own secret.

"I know you have premonitions, it's difficult not to pay attention to it when unusual circumstances kept happening. I know about the day you were attacked, you were not bitten by a vampire or scratched by a werewolf. You were shot with an experimental drug and helped a little with magic. Our fathers were best friends, they were a part of the same order and unfortunately others knew they were both shapeshifters, my mother was one of the Fae fairies. Your mother was introduced to your father by my mother, she was a Fae also. They hoped by not teaching you, the power inside you would go away. If it's not used it gets extremely weak, it might be there but not enough to do something. When you were attacked, it came out and because of it I was able to heal you. I went looking for my date when I realized something was wrong, it was a feeling I couldn't shake and it was a good thing, you were lying there dying. I helped get your body's healing process started. I became the leader of the group intentionally, but they don't know it's me, I've always been under a mask and am much stronger than the others, majority of them are witches, and I impressed and made them fearful enough of me not to question me. When a couple revolted and tried to take over, I taught them a lesson none of them would forget, no one has gone after me since. I knew a few of them had been creating experiments but nothing they would show me, they hid them, and I hoped they would slip up, but they were always incredibly careful. They remembered your past but forgot about me, so I had to try and link myself to you." Skylar stopped for a moment waiting to see how I was taking it.

"Micheal is my younger brother, why wouldn't they take him also, wouldn't he be the same as myself?" I felt strange asking and hoped he wasn't waiting and being held captive waiting for me.

"He never uses his gifts, it's not that he couldn't strengthen them but if you don't know they are there, it's the last thing you will resort to, so they must have assumed he didn't inherit anything. I made sure he had the main tracker; he can find us using his cell phone. I made sure he was holding onto it when he left. If anything happens to him and it doesn't read his fingerprint when its being used, mine will glow red which thankfully it hasn't. Yours would do the same. Right now, we need to find a better area for shelter, the wind is picking up and there's lightning in the distance." Skylar nodded towards where we came from.

We kept walking through the thick forest, it was incredibly overgrown by vines taking over the bushes and trees. There hadn't been a path, but we kept going in one direction hoping to put more space between us and the others. The rain started to downpour as we picked up the pace and walked faster until we were in a full-on run. There was an alcove up ahead and it would have to be enough for tonight. Once we were there, we pulled out the smaller loose trees and stacking them up trying to close off the outside weather. The ground was already soft so pulling them out was rather easy. We were able to gather enough to cut down on the wind and rain. There were leaves that were still dry, starting a fire by rubbing a few sticks together from friction, we were careful the direction and how high the smoke went. The last thing we needed them to see was the smoke from staying warm.

We sat there quietly for a while watching the rain pour down. Being here with Skylar brought back memories of when our families used to go camping with each other. The three of us were partners in crime, if there was something to get into and get in trouble, it was usually us three doing it. We never hesitated to adventure, even if we might get injured, we were willing to try. One thing that hasn't changed is how Skylar took charge, she did it when we were little and still does it now. I couldn't help but smile.

"What is that dopey smile for?" Skylar asked.

"I was thinking about when we used to go camping, Micheal and I never questioned that you knew what you were doing and followed you blindly, even when we got hurt. I fell down that long cliff or Micheal took the wrong step onto a branch and fell breaking his arm because you said it was safe." It wasn't the only thing I was thinking about.

"I think I loved it most when we found that hole by the tree that we thought was an animal home only to find there was an abandoned mining shaft. There was a lot of equipment still in there." Skylar seemed rather happy reminiscing.

"Did you know about me back then? I'm curious why you knew, and my parents never shared with me any of this. I'm shocked you never told us. You always told me everything especially when it was overtelling me things I never wanted to know." She told me so many things I wished she had kept to herself, especially the first time she compared me to how a fish might kiss.

"I've always known so I assume my parents probably said something at some point, but I never gave it any thought, it wasn't something we sat around talking about. My parents were determined to train me and my sister when she was alive, when she passed all of that stopped, I was taught not to let anyone know about any of my gifts and I was to keep them secret at all costs because it wasn't only keeping my family and myself safe, but yours as well." Skylar kept looking outward.

"I wish I knew where they took us, actually I wish I had a phone so I could call my brother. He must be wondering what's going on." I kept hoping he was safe.

It rained extremely hard for a few hours but once it started to lighten to barely a drizzle, we scattered the small trees we used for shelter all around otherwise it would have been an easy indicator that we were here. We kept walking in one direction. Landscaping was changing to more of a hilly region where we were constantly going up or down a hill. We crossed a few streams and followed along a mini lake with a rocky shore. Skylar was rather determined in the direction she was going, especially when she changed course slightly, not curving back but going to the right a little.

"Do you know where you're going or are we just sightseeing without the benefit of taking our time?" I was curious what she was thinking.

"My father told me if we were ever in trouble to go here, I had a feeling we were not far and it's because this area conducts a special energy unground which is probably what they were trying to tap into. If your parents had trained you then you would be able to sense this place and find it." She kept walking as she explained.

"Can they find this place if you can sense it?" I didn't want to have them join us if it was that much of a target.

"Bears mark their territory, either by the scent glands in their feet, anal glands or scratches on trees. The scratches anyone could notice but we most likely won't pick up on the other except animals would. It's sort of like that but not as gross, our families have a rather scent to distinguish from one another, whether you wish to call it a potion, artificial liquid or magic, it's what we as family pick up on. So only we should find it. It's a place your parents have been to also." She talked as she ducked under a branch that slapped me right in the face.

"Thanks for the branch. Is it that overwhelming smell of berries? I keep smelling then but when I look around, I don't see any, maybe pinecones and a few of those Holly berries and usually I don't smell those." I noticed the scent getting stronger the longer we walked.

"Is this the first time you've noticed something like this?" Skylar looked back at me for a moment.

"Not really, there were other strange things, but I couldn't exactly figure them out. I've been aware there was something off about myself and I was able to do things, I figured if I was able to, then I wasn't going to stop myself, but I was careful around people I didn't trust." I loved the strength part, but I did wish I didn't get tired.

"Because you've been using your gifts, it's why they are not as weak for you as they normally would be. When we get a chance to, I want to teach you and Micheal how to use your gifts." Skylar kept leading the way.

"How much further, I don't know about you but I'm tired, we traveled for a full day with them and since the sun is about to go back down, I'm tired." I didn't want to sound whiny, but I couldn't stop yawning and I already swallowed a fly because of it.

"I promise we are rather close now, just over that rope bridge and we will be there." Skylar pointed across the way.

The bridge she pointed out wasn't exactly a bridge, there were ropes on either side but nothing to step on. Once we were next to it, I wondered how we were going to balance unless we walked sideways holding onto one side, at least if one of us swayed it wouldn't interrupt the other side. There was a small rope laying near the floor area, pulling on it, there was a quick zip sound as it pulled along a thick mesh in the center. There was space enough to pull it back and forth like a draw string curtain. Stepping onto it, the rope did sway but was rather strong. Walking across it slowly, we made it to the other side. I only looked down once, it was rather steep, something I never cared for was high places. Once across the rope bridge, Skylar pulled another rope on this side pulling the center back to this side. We walked even further into the woods; the ground was rocky as we made our way. There was a cabin tucked in a rock wall. At least the front resembled a small, abandoned cabin but inside it was all carved out with several rooms, the center hallway gradually lowered down to a second and third floor.

"We should be safe here; I wish I had my phone, when they cut my clothes off, my phone was in the pocket. I tried to bring it with me, but they took it saying they didn't want us being distracted and any clothing would be saved for us in a bag with our name on it in the main ballroom. I had to hide my tracker in my hair, thank goodness they never checked us, or they would have taken out my hair clips or they would have found it. I think they assumed the clips were plastic, it was the metals they were trying to keep out of the end room." Skylar parted her long hair and lifted it slightly to pull out the tracker she had clipped in.

"Does the flashing mean Micheal isn't safe?" I was worried but couldn't remember what she said earlier, I was easily distracted.

"It's flashing green which means it's being tracked by Micheal; I doubt he's close enough yet so right now it will only let us know he's looking for us. If someone else is using the signal it will show up as red to let us know there is an urgency, I hope if it happens your bother will be more cautious and protect himself." Skylar walked down to the third door while waving for me to join her.

Following her into the room, it looked like a very girlish room. Soft pink, fluffy fuzz on the walls, purple fuzzy carpet, metal plate with several candles on it with matches next to it. She unzipped the plastic protective sheet from the bed, setting it to the side of the bed and pulling back the blanket.

"Whoever stayed in here had quite the imagination and was certainly an interesting person." I wasn't sure what to say, I felt like a fell into a little girl's dream room.

"I know you saying 'it's interesting' is your way of saying you don't like it. I was a little kid when I was last here, I liked everything fuzzy, it's when we found our cat fuzzers. I admit I went overboard with it and my parents indulged it and I turned out perfectly fine. We can sleep here for now and hopefully finish working our way back to your brother, or we can hide in here when he finds us and try to figure out what we are going to do with the order. At some point we will have to deal with them again, but I want to be prepared." Skylar slipped her shoes off and slipped under the covers.

"I'll stay awake for now and we'll switch like we did last time." I was going to leave the room until Skylar called me.

"It's safe for both of us to sleep. I set the alarm once we came in, it was by the door, small enough I know it's there but not enough for someone unfamiliar with the place to have seen it. I admit the comforter smelled like fresh apples, after being closed up for so long, the sachet bag on the top kept the scent." Skylar lifted the one side for me to join.

Slipping under the blanket, I felt like a kid again. When we were little, we would make blanket forts and would play for so long we didn't bother getting under the blankets, we all fell asleep on top of the bed, never worried about anything, especially the future.

"Remember when we used to hide under the blanket thinking our parents couldn't see us. There were times they played along and as we found out, they left to eat out for dinner, and we had fallen asleep waiting for them to find us." There were so many memories of us as kids.

"I don't mean to make things depressing, but I always wondered what happened to your parents. None of this makes sense. Experimenting with sex is certainly a way to get attention and maybe for some it helps lower their guard, but it didn't seem like they used it for everyone. Nude bodies would be easier to replicate since clothing can be added later but the power, they seem to have was far more advanced than I thought they were." Skylar was busy trying to figure it out.

"Micheal and I never knew what happened to them. One day we said goodbye on our way to school, we were told our uncle would be picking us up, mom seemed a little more emotional than normal but at the time I didn't think anything of it until now. Our uncle never picked us up. We had an inheritance from our parents, and I grew up quick, I had to be the parent, no one else checked on us so we finished raising ourselves. We were already seventeen. I don't know which one, but I assume it was Akuma, she said you etched your history and sacred symbols in me when she would have rather seen me die, what happened at that time, other than feeling like I was on fire, I don't remember much." I hoped she might tell me.

"I knew they wanted to kill you, and I didn't know if it would work so I scribed the sigils into your body, they were of an ancient language. The order has several sacred books but there is one in particular that they rarely let anyone get close enough to. I needed to get close to it, so I dressed as a man and impressed them with my gifts, after several years and horrible tests, they trusted me. They never once thought it was me who stole the book, there was another member who said they did but they were angry at the order for something and they killed him, they never knew where the book was. When I scribed the words on your skin, instead of staying on the outside, they were absorbed exactly as I hoped they would. Each word your body took in and then disappeared from the book. No one could access the pages anymore. I'm hoping one day you will be able to, and I think it's what they are hoping for. They think by keeping your friend, meaning me and your brother alive, you might be more willing to work with them. I mainly joined because I was trying to find out who killed my parents and to find out what happened with yours." Skylar looked worried.

"Micheal and I have a lot of questions, I wish you could have let me know more about this earlier, I worry that you put yourself in so much danger." I always worried when she was alone.

"I know you've always been protective of me and I'm thankful for that, but I doubt I could have pretended to be the male they needed, there were a lot of things I couldn't have done if either of you knew." Skylar sighed.

"I know you well enough to know you hate keeping secrets from your best friends, and it shows from the way you start acting. Especially when you're tired. You keep yawning and need sleep; we both do since we don't know how tomorrow is going to be and I don't know where Micheal is either. I'm hoping he's safe. Let's get sleep while we have a chance to." Hugging Skylar and giving her a kiss on the forehead,

Snuggling close to each other, it hadn't taken either of us long to fall asleep, I kept my arm over her, I wasn't risking her leaving or being taken without my knowing it. I was still worried about both of us sleeping even though we needed it but Skylar seemed to think it was safe enough place to be.

# Chapter Nine

It felt good waking up next to Skylar. I wished there was a way to contact my brother, I had no idea if he was trying to find us or if they might have grabbed him, possibly never letting him leave when we last saw him. Skylar smiled at me as she woke up.

"You look worried, I told you we were safe here." Skylar looked concerned.

"I know you said we were safe, but we need to find a way of contacting Micheal, its driving me crazy not knowing if he's safe or not." I knew we couldn't hide forever.

"There's a town near here, we could use the phone to find out where he's at and make sure he meets us here. It would be safer than either of our homes in town even though I worry about our animals. I know we have timed feeders, so they will be okay for a little while." Skylar started to get nervous.

Reluctantly getting out of bed, I would have preferred spending more time here, but we had certain things to do first. Skylar grabbed cash that her family hid in the cabin before we left. I followed Skylar since she knew the direction of where the town was. I still felt lost. I remembered the cabin and many years of memories, but I never remember getting here, usually I was asleep in the backseat of the car on our way here.

Walking for an hour or more, I swear when we were in town I wanted to buy a watch, it was bothering me not knowing what day or time it was. I had gotten used to the most basic of technology even if it didn't seem like much. The cabin didn't have electricity, phones or anything connected to it. Skylar was correct, the town wasn't too far and it was smaller than the one we grew up in. A couple of stores and dirt roads leading off in various directions, one had a sign pointing towards the local school. Going into one of the general stores, Skylar picked out a couple food and drink items for us, while I used their phone to call

Micheal. It rang several times before going to his answering machine. I wanted to keep the message cryptic in case the order kept our phones and were watching any texts or messages we were sent.

"You can already guess who this is, hopefully you can find us, best childhood memories cabin, I'll try calling again later." Hanging up the phone, I felt more nervous worrying what might have happened to him.

"If they have him most likely they would bring him here. I have a few things; we will wait at the cabin and can inspect the compound later tonight once its dark." Skylar whispered to me.

No one seemed to be watching us or curious if we were new. We still watched to be careful not to be followed. We made our long walk back in silence not wanting to risk being heard either. Still no signs of my brother coming but I did wonder if he would know where this place was. He had a better memory than I did but still, it's been middle school since we were last here. I wondered why Skylar chose to walk through the woods rather than take the barely seen two track into town. Once we were in, I watched as she set the alarm, something that I easily missed the first time.

Skylar put the food away and kept walking around checking different cupboards and then said she was going outside, for me to stay put until she came back in. Watching her flip the security switch again when she went out. I was curious what she was doing and not very patient since my fight or flight was constantly going since we took off yesterday. I doubted they would try anything when people could be seen easily during the daylight, but I didn't like risking having Skylar out of my eyesight for too long. Then the door opened, and she reset the alarm. Grabbing my hand, she led me to the hallway closet and showed me a panel that as in there. She flipped the switch, and I could hear the appliances start up.

"How do we have power?" I was surprised.

"This old place has several backup generators, my parents insisted on keeping several, that way we never needed an actual electrical line to be brought back here. It can run the well, septic and thankfully the shower. It's going to be a little colder tonight so having the heat on will be nice. There are several solar panels up above a few of the trees, they wouldn't get much down here on the ground under all these trees. Give me a few minutes and meet me in the bathroom." Skylar didn't wait for an answer as she left me standing there.

I turned the little television on but found the signal too weak, so I turned it back off. I hoped I might find the local news. It was extremely bright out and we had several hours to fill before we looked around.

Looking at the bookshelf, there were several from my parents. Pulling down one that said geographical science. I knew I never would have been interested in this when I was a kid but would read it now. Instead, there were no pages, it was a fake book. The key was taped on the inside cover, so they were not trying hard to keep anyone out. Unlocking it and opening it up, it revealed a smaller journal which happened to be in my mother's handwriting. Flipping through the pages, it described both of us growing up, places we had been, a few 'developments' of ours they chose not to let us know about. Apparently, Micheal when he was five, he shifted through the wall but was too excited to be outside playing never paid attention to it, or when I had seen a bird and was upset it flew away, that I shifted into a bird and flew around with it. I had given my mother a personal heart attack when she was worried, I would shift back and realize I was falling and panic. There were a few comments about how thankful she was that we were sound sleepers, or it would have been more difficult for the adult games they had planned. Apparently, Hazel and Joseph, Skylar's parents were rather bold playing hide the rubber ball on a string. That next time they were going to liven things up a bit by using a handmade toy that vibrated. I couldn't believe what I was reading, were they swingers?

"Gregory." Skylar called me.

Placing the book back, I went to see what she wanted. Stepping into the bathroom, there was so much steam, there were two robes hanging on the wall, a change of clothes for both of us.

"It will definitely feel good to take a shower. You can take yours first since you set this whole thing up." I was about to leave when she grabbed my arm.

"You're showering with me." Skylar pushed the door closed and pulled me to the center of the room.

She pulled my shirt up over my head and dropped it on the floor, then she pulled my sweatpants down letting them drop around my angles. Sliding her hands along my sides and she slowly slipped my underwear off, letting those drop to the ground.

"Do you think this is a good idea right now?" Not that I would turn her down.

"I heard no protesting as I took your clothes off and if you're willing to have those men have their way with what should be mine, then yes, it's a good idea, besides it's not as if it's our first time." She pulled her shirt off showing she wasn't wearing a bra and dropped her sweatpants to the floor.

"This would be the first time we've had sex." I felt nervous saying that as she led me into the shower.

The shower had a dual head, one on either side of the shower and a small sprayer on the back part of the wall. The water felt incredibly comfortable. I could see she was busy; she cleaned the entire shower. The shower was large enough to fit five people so if our parents were getting intimate with each other, they would have fit in here.

"We both know that isn't true. You have a rather distinctive scent. So even if you don't talk, I know when it's you, my date came extremely late, untied me and went to bed. I knew it was you who made out with me, you were rather fresh for thinking I would never know. I admit, I enjoyed the surprise especially since I wasn't expecting it." Skylar grabbed the liquid soap and poured it into her hand.

"I didn't think you knew since you didn't say anything." I could feel my cheeks blush.

Standing behind me, she started to rub me from the shoulders down, slowly enjoying touching me as she went rubbing down to my ass as she caressed it, slipping her hand between my buttocks.

"It looked so sexy when he had you pinned, and he was thrusting in you. I wanted to feel how tight you were." Skylar whispered to me.

Rinsing off my bottom, she pulled back my cheeks and nuzzled slightly as she licked the rim of my anus, slowly adding pressure with her tongue. She slightly dipped her tongue in, and I let out a light moan. The soft, wet feeling of her tongue was turning me on. She licked around a little more before she moved on.

She kept soaping me up while rubbing down my lower legs, then she slipped between my legs to be in front, she grabbed my scrotum and scrubbed around it, sliding her other hand along my penis. Letting the water rinse it off, she took part of it in her mouth, licking around the tip, and sliding her tongue down the shaft felt amazing. She squeezed at one end while she would place her mouth around and let it go slightly further into her mouth. I kept getting quick dizzy moments from the feeling. Then she stopped and stood up now soaping my stomach and up to my chest.

Coming up to my mouth, she licked my lips before kissing them. She firmly planted her lips on mine, then pulled away with my lower lip between her teeth. I took the soap and turned her around. Massaging down her back, I slipped forward to rub her breasts before coming to her back again. Running my hands down, I kneeled as I massaged the rim of her anus with the soap, rinsing it off, I pressed a little with my thumb, then I pressed my tongue against it, slipping in slowly I added pressure by lifting my chin slightly pushing the tongue up more. She seemed to like this. Pulling my tongue out, I soaped up her legs. I stayed on my knees as I moved to the front of her, rubbing my soapy hand between her labia, around her vagina and slipping a couple fingers in. Rinsing the soap off I licked around her labia, sucking on it lightly at first and then sucked at her firmly. Placing four fingers directly into her vagina, I thrust them up and down quickly. I could feel her squeezing my hand slightly. I did this a few more times before stopping and standing back up. I continued to kiss her on the lips. I don't know why I wondered if our parents had sex in here, it wasn't the greatest thought, but my brain tended to go elsewhere it didn't belong.

"You seem distracted?" Skylar asked.

"Sorry, I don't want to ruin the mood." I started to kiss her neck.

"I'm sure it won't ruin my mood, what were you thinking?" As she asked, she turned off the shower.

"I think our parents were swingers with each other. I found a journal of my mom's in a fake book, and I was reading it, there were enough odd comments that make it sound like that." I still wasn't sure how to take it.

"Our parents were part of the free love hippie fun. There's quite a bit I could show you." Grabbing our towels we dried off.

Once we were dressed, instead of going back to our room, she brought me down another level to another room. The room was rather large with tremendously obvious sex toys and furniture.

"Why did I never know this was done here?" I felt shocked to see it.

"Because we were not allowed down to the lower third floor. This is a typical sex dungeon. They had fun, there are a ton of videos, pictures, toys. There are some great books down here. I could have fun torturing you down here. When they were first a part of the order, it was much more relaxed, nothing like it is now. They wanted to have fun, experiment and enjoy not only their magic but how using the energy from each other would affect things. At first, I thought Akuma wanted to create sex toys made from water which would have been fine, and I know you had the same idea, but she wanted to make them more lifelike, beyond the cold stone faces they have now. They don't seem to last as long but once they do and I have a feeling she's figured out how to do that and it involves us somehow. I don't think her intent is good. When water bursts, it shouldn't evaporate into dust, whatever was in the water in that lake has something to do with it. She could even replace the real people eventually." As she spoke, she pulled me over to a cabinet.

Opening it up, there were whips, chains, various long or thick dildo's, soft and hard rubber balls that either were regular or vibrated with a long strip on them. Skylar grabbed from the new items that were still in plastic bags, three of the balls with string, then grabbed lavender oil and a few more toys. Taking my hand and bringing me over to the mat. She took the protective cover off. I wasn't sure if I was going to like it but if Skylar was turned on by it. I would pretty much do anything she wanted. However, I was hesitant by one of the items she picked out and made sure to set it next to me.

"Are you sure you want to use that?" I hoped she wasn't going to use the huge dildo; I did make it clear I wasn't gay, I'm not exactly the type to ask other men if they liked this and I assumed gay men did.

"Yes, it's all necessary, she kept placing items around me almost like I was the center piece of an offering.

I trusted Skylar beyond anything, but I was wondering what I got myself into this time. Skylar had me lay down on my stomach as she held my hands behind my back using soft handcuffs to keep them there. I hadn't been paying attention except I felt my ankles being shackled as well, did she think I was going to fight her on this? I felt her pour oil on my backside letting some of it drip down the sides. She started to massage my buttocks, squeezing them, running her thumbs between them and rather close to my anus. Skylar was using a strap on as she oiled it up, then she slowly pressed against the rim. Small pokes at first until the tip was in. I had to remind myself to relax, and it would go in easier which wasn't easy since it kept pinching. Skylar rested her legs on either side of mine and leaned over me slightly before asking me.

"I'm going to ask you a few questions and I want you to answer them, each time you don't answer correctly, I'll add a little pain or experiment a little firmer with your body." Skylar stated.

"You know you can ask me anything." I wasn't sure what she would want to ask me.

"How long have you been interested in me?" She said.

"I don't know, I think this whole game we got involved in brought it out." I didn't want to say from childhood, how would she know?

"Wrong answer." She pressed into me as the dildo went in a little but not all the way yet.

"I've known you had a crush on me for a long time, how long have you wanted to have sex with me." Skylar whispered this time.

"I honestly don't know when, I was too young when I had my first crush on you, I wasn't thinking of sex until much later. Probably when we were in high school." I hoped she would believe me.

"Sounds more like you, Micheal said you have visions and kept one that involves me but chose to keep it from me. What was it?" She asked again.

"You don't want to know, they change so it's difficult to say if it's going to happen, especially if I can change something to temporarily change the end. I've seen it change from you to another person. It all depends on what is happening at the time." I truly hadn't wanted to tell her.

"Wrong answer again." She said.

She thrust harder forcing the dildo in all the way until it stopped not going in anymore. I jerked slightly from not expecting it. Taking a deep breath, I expected her to do it again, instead she kept it in but wiggled back and forth a little.

"Do you not want me concerned about you?" I tried to sound as sincere as I felt.

"I love that you care but when it's about my life, even if it doesn't happen, I want to know. I know you've tried to hide it but far too often it happens. I have a right to know." She gave another shove.

"I promise I'll tell you but right now doesn't feel like the best time. Are you enjoying this?" I was curious if she was going to use the thick dildo that was a few inches from my face and hoping not.

"Yes, I am enjoying it, I like how you flinch. I can see why men like this, the full control, thrusting hard enough to make your partner flinch, how your body reacts to it." Skylar spoke as she pulled her hips back allowing the strap on to come out a little and then pushed back quickly.

She started to grind back and forth, pushing upward slightly, getting the most reaction from me, she repeated it, and a few times pulled almost all the way out and then thrust back in with quite a bit of power. She was extremely enjoying this.

"Nice way to work the glutes, I see you haven't used the fun toy yet, it hurts going in the first time but after that it's an easy ride." Micheal slapped one of Skylar's buttocks.

"How did you get in without the alarm going off? Grab us a towel." Last thing I wanted was my brother watching me have sex.

"I turned the alarm off when I got here but it's turned on again. When I say I'm going on vacation, this is usually where that is, great private place, lots of toys, I usually thoroughly enjoy my date and they get a few in also, never hurts to be bottoms up sometimes. The girls can be quite creative, gotta love the pain sometimes. Looks like you have him strapped down good enough he's not going anywhere, try one of my favorites, it vibrates. Just grind on him with it and you'll have an orgasm also." Micheal went over to a drawer and pulled out a dildo to add onto the strap on.

"Thanks for giving her ideas, you don't need to be here to watch," I hoped he would leave, thankful Micheal's okay but not wanting him here right now.

"You're welcome, what are younger hornier brothers for? Besides, I'm enjoying the back view." Micheal made no intention of leaving the room, sitting behind Skylar to watch her.

The dildo he handed Skylar was larger and with a fast vibration. Removing the smaller one and replacing it with a thicker one, it wasn't smooth like the other one, this one was ribbed which would slow down the thrusting. Oiling it up and pressing it to my anus, it certainly didn't slide in like the other one. I started to think if she were to use her fist it would still be smaller, Skylar was determined to get it in, once the tip was in, it took a while of her coaxing it back and forth before she got it to go in, at the base she pushed the round button, and it started to vibrate. My legs tightened as I tried to stretch out, she pushed it in further until it was all the way in. laying on me, she had her legs on either side as she grinded on my ass, back and forth slowly.

"Mmmm, this does feel good." Skylar said as she raised her bottom a little.

"I am not having sex with my brother." I was worried when I could barely see my brother stand behind Skylar.

"The last thing I would want is to have sex with my brother either, that's gross. Not to worry, I'm only here to make it more uncomfortable for you and pleasurable for the lady. The new dildo has various speeds, so if you thought this was fast, wait till you try the others. I have the controller for the one inside of the strap on so I can control Skylar's pleasure." Micheal teased.

Micheal licked Skylar's anus as she kept grinding, I could feel her gripping more with her legs. The vibration kept changing as Micheal played with the settings on both of ours. They did this for another few minutes until Skylar had her orgasm and one last rough thrust into me with the strap on.

# Chapter Ten

Micheal was out in the living room with a video playing on the television. Skylar watched me get dressed in the bedroom. She walked over to me with her hand going down into my pants grabbing my penis.

"Next time I promise, you can do anything you want with me." She whispered and kissed my ear.

"I'm going to keep you to that promise." I certainly planned on having fun with her but not with Micheal watching.

For now, we both went out to find out how Micheal was and if he knew anything about the order. He turned the television off once we joined him. Sitting on the couch and getting comfortable.

"I never knew this was where you took your time off. Why don't I remember this place, I remember small moments but not this place?" I knew we took a lot of vacations as kids but the memories of this place outside weren't coming to me.

"You can thank mom for that. She did something to you in the kitchen. When we were playing outside, you blew a hole through the wall which is why the far left one looks different from the others. They didn't want you to remember, they must not have realized I saw it. I didn't want to forget the way you did so I hid any special gifts that I had. Even the order underestimated me assuming I didn't inherit any gifts from our parents thinking I was ordinary. I did collect your phones for you, the clothes were heaped in a pile with everyone else's, but the phones were on the side, I only found those easily because Skylar has pink fuzzy fur with bear designs on hers and yours is all black with a starry background and the black eye galaxy design with a large letter G." Leaning forward from his chair, Micheal handed us both back our phones.

"I'm missing a few apps on my phone. And it's in airplane mode. Probably check through it to make sure they didn't put a tracker on them." Skylar was looking through everything to see what they were looking for.

"They obviously searched your phones, I put then on airplane mode before I came here so they couldn't track me coming this way. I also refilled the animal's feeders at both of your places so they will last three more days, as a side note Greogry, your cat is a demon, he attacked me the second I came in the house." Micheal was pleased with himself.

Lifting his pant leg, Micheal showed the long deep scratches left behind by Otis.

"I'll have to reward Otis when we get back, he might be a better guard then the dog." For being considered unadoptable, he's fitting in just fine.

"I think it's strange they would rearrange my photos, there is a new folder. Its only showing vials filled with something and I know I never took these." Micheal looked confused.

"It looks like syringes and vials on mine, why would they want us to see these? There must be a reason otherwise they would not have added these." Skylar sounded confused.

"If you look closer at a few of your personal photos, they have added a few members to make it look like they were there when in reality they never were, its pretty good photoshop." I added.

The people added were not ones we knew but neither did they have expressions on their faces, one of the pictures had everyone smiling and there were two people added but neither showed any expression at all, they looked dead inside, so we guessed they hadn't added real people but water creations.

"Maybe they want people to get used to the way they look so they won't think differently when they get introduced to the world." Skylar was still examining her pictures.

"Before I came here, I checked out the cave, it's been emptied so I don't think they plan on using it anymore. The ground was brushed to cover any footprints" Micheal said.

"We know where their next area is, but it's not easy to get to. We were planning on investigating it once the sun went down so we could hide better in the dark. We were worried they grabbed you or worse." Skylar looked worried as she looked at Micheal.

"Nope, they had no interest in me other than asking where your favorite places were, they must have been looking for you at that point." Micheal kept giving me a strange look.

"Speaking of people dying, you never did tell me, we were interrupted by your brother, otherwise I would have tortured you longer." Skylar demanded.

"I never make a promise not that I wanted to tell you. My premonitions are not always clear but many times after they happen, they make more sense when I can see the other parts that were missing that made it happen. I kept seeing you lying on a marble floor inside an expensive house dying, you were laying in a pool of blood. In your hand, you're holding a torn red piece of red satin. We didn't have those types of estates in the little town where we live which is why I worried the entire time you were gone, but when I was around others, I kept seeing it, except it wasn't you who died, when I didn't have anyone around, I would see it more often and it was you." I felt confused as to how having others physically around me affected it.

"Maybe you're the missing component," Micheal looked and me regretting he said it, "you know I'm always wrong but maybe people use you to get closer to Skylar? If they think your gay, they would think you're the safe friend to suck up to thinking you would put in a good word for them." Micheal wondered.

"I still don't see why they were using sex as one of the party themes, anyone can get hot and horny if it's done right, some religious groups feel the energy used during it can strengthen the power of something they are working on. Unless I'm over thinking this?" Skylar asked.

"You're definitely over thinking it, I would have loved having it as one of the reasons I was at the party, so far, they were all word guessing or association games. I thought those were better for Gregory since he used to play those for hours." Micheal joked.

"He definitely had a surprise, I'm thankful to have been able to watch, yes I'm going to let your brother know, when we had the two-way mirror, that guy was going to town on you and it looked like you were enjoying it, especially once you saw me." Skylar bumped into me slightly.

"Since I was tied up, I assumed everyone was having this done, I figured once it was done, I would move on to another room. I'm always willing to try something once." I didn't want to admit it happened twice.

"At least you haven't admitted if you like or hated it, many men like it but won't admit to it because of the stigma unless they are gay and even then, a few have issues with it. I don't mind it, the good old juicy meat cradled between soft buns, creamy cheese nestled in fresh bread, and a sizzling hotdog perfectly snuggled in its fluffy bun!" Micheal laughed.

"I think I'll be vegetarian for a while." I stated.

"I lost my libido. I think I'll check if its dark enough out yet."

Skylar stood up and walked over to the window, looking out looking disappointed it was still too light out.

"I'm not saying I'm attracted to men, I'm after women but if things get kinky, I'll do anything, kind of like your try anything once Gregory." Smiling, Micheal knew he got to me.

"Now that Micheal is here, do we still want to investigate? What are we going to do if we find anything?" At this point I wasn't sure what we could do.

"Other than the fact you were taken hostage, going to the party was one thing but forced to an unknown location and having to escape is an illegal move. But since their place is such a strong bunker, I want to know what is down there, but I didn't want to be trapped there, at least this way I control what happens we might find something in there that will help us figure out what we are going to do." Skylar stated.

"Before I left town, there were more of those ashes being found in dumpsters around town, so far people are keeping it quiet hoping not to panic anyone but there has to be a reason they are doing it, otherwise they could dump it anywhere in the woods or back in the water and no one would know since it would blow away in the wind." Micheal stated.

"Skylar, do they still think the person you used to shift into is still relevant?" I was curious if she could pretend to be the other person still.

"They do but his power is getting limited, Akuma wants more control without anyone else knowing exactly what she's doing, she doesn't share all of it with her twin sister, not that she seems to care. Akuma doesn't work or play well with others, she's a control freak and would rather not deal with anyone. At least that was how she was when I got to know her." Skylar stated.

"Both of you could stay here and I could go on my own, that way I can get in and out quick." I hoped this way I could keep everyone else safe.

"Pretty much hand over what they want? Skylar is stronger than you since she's used her gifts since childhood, and I'm used to hiding what I can do and I'm stronger than you, if anyone is getting left behind it would be you, I do admit all three of us would stand out more which isn't a good thing." Micheal stated.

"I know a lot of their secrets but this one they've kept from me; I want to know what is going on in there. Eisheth has always been silent, she doesn't like to speak, I sometimes wondered if Akuma did something to her, she's usually very flighty and she keeps to herself. Akuma can be manipulative but never underestimate her, she's smarter than she lets you believe. Gregory, when you met with the mystery person in the cave, did you ever see who it was?" Skylar asked.

"Micheal and I went back later when we were going to confront them, but they were doing a ritual by the water and it was the first time we saw the water creatures, they led them into the cave, and they closed it off. I only heard one of the girls speaking so I don't know which one it was." I couldn't tell the two apart from a distance other than one looked an inch taller than the other and one kept her hands in her pockets the whole time.

"Akuma is the only one who talks, I know you don't want to hear this and you are not the most patient when it comes to waiting, but I think if would be better if Micheal and I went in. You'll be safe here." Skylar spoke Softley knowing I wasn't going to like it.

"You're right, I don't want to hear it, and I want to keep you safe also, it would also be difficult to explain why both of us are with you. I hate the idea of staying behind, but if you take too long then I'll come looking for both of you." I stated.

They knew me well enough to know I would be restless and worried until I knew they were both safe, especially since they were going back into that place Skylar had us leave intentionally. I didn't feel good about this but at least my vision wasn't coming back to me. I had to trust that they would be alright. We watched as Micheal filled a backpack with items, he thought they might need while they were gone. Once it became dark enough, I gave both my brother and Skylar a hug and watched them disappear into the night. Closing the door, I had no idea how I was going to occupy myself until they were back, other than to explore this place, there were several more rooms I wasn't familiar with. There were four floors and six rooms off each. The main rooms we stayed in were on the first floor, the hallway led down gradually until it came to a staircase that went led off to different floors. I always thought the first floor was odd, you could look over the rail only to see the hallway disappear underneath.

The second floor had the impressive shower, larger bedrooms that were reserved for our parents, nothing out of the ordinary there. Each bedroom had a shower. What I was impressed by was the fact there was no power coming into this place but there was a building out back that controlled all the power used to run this place.

The first room on the third floor had a bunch of science books collecting dust, beakers, test tubes, Microscope, volumetric flask, Bunsen burner, burette, funnels, ammeter, crucible, magnets, rulers, incubators, spatula. I was surprised to find how stocked the room was, it was a fully functional laboratory with an emergency eye wash station and a mini shower in the corner. There was a bookcase on the far side of the room filled with books, with one pulled out a slight bit further than the others. Attempting to pull it out to see what someone was looking at, the lower half didn't budge but the upper half tilted toward me, and I heard a click. Putting my hand on the side of the bookcase, I was able to pull it towards me, revealing a room behind it. All three walls were lined with shelves filled with jars, the center of the room had filing cabinets, each filled with specimens preserved in special slides. Several empty petri dishes were scattered in one of the drawers. I was surprised to see a chromatography machine set up on the left side of the room, these machines were used to precisely separate and purify different chemicals. There were no chemicals left over, nothing stored in the fridge in the corner, the plug had been pulled out of the socket. Everything had been used but there wasn't anything to give you an idea of what they were being used for.

I was curious if Skylar knew about this room, she knew the place better than I had and I know my brother would have snooped but why wouldn't he tell me if he knew. I kept searching the other rooms, most of them were empty. On the fourth floor there was only one large room with all types of exercise equipment, in the right corner was an older style wet sauna, a hot tub in the other corner next to a large empty tub used for ice baths. A large cart held towels of various sizes, water bottles and exercise mats. Back behind the stairs was a large shower area made with seven shower heads and viewable from all angles.

I wished my parents were around, I had so many questions for them and how did I forget or not know all of this was down here, was it part of their making me forget? What was it they used to get me to forget, it wasn't simply one thing, it made me forget a lot of others as well around that time. If Micheal was careful not to get caught, I wondered if he knew exactly what they did or if he simply knew something was happening. I had a lot of questions for him when he got back also.

Since they left, this was the first time that I thought of them. I guessed by now they should be close to the order. This time they had their cell phones on them, and I had mine, all three of us had them in silence mode so they would not go off at the wrong time. If they needed me, I knew they would call me, not that phone connection was that great out here. I felt completely helpless waiting here hoping everything was going to be okay.

# Chapter Eleven

Making our way through the woods towards the deep pit, it looked like they hadn't replaced the water or whatever was stored in there. This was going to make it more difficult for Micheal and me to get across but at least it wouldn't be obvious we were here having duplicates made of us. The ones that formed earlier of Gregory and me must have already been collected. Micheal opened the backpack he grabbed from the house and pulled out a rope, tying it to a nearby tree and running it through the bushes to keep it from standing out, he lowered the other end for us to climb down.

"I know you're a good climber, we can get down, but we will have to find another way up. Before we do, there's a dark corner over there I want to check out, depending on what it is we might be able to use it." Micheal pointed in the direction he was looking.

"If we had two ropes I would race you down." Skylar waited for Micheal to go first.

This wasn't a natural pond or area carved out by water, the area was too flat below and along the outer wall, the center area was rather jagged up top but down below it was also incredibly smooth. Looking around the sides there hadn't been any visible security cameras. The dark area was a little deeper than the rest of the area with steps leading down. Walking down slightly there was a door, we assumed once the fake water transformed, they were planning on having the people come through this door. Trying the handle, it was locked. Micheal took out a few pins from the bag and messed with the handle. It wasn't a key lock but there was a hole in the center, pushing a pin through the hole, it unlocked rather easily. They probably assumed no one would find it while it was under water before.

Being careful of what could be on the other side of the door, Micheal pushed it open before entering to see if anything was there. We hadn't seen anyone. Taking a few steps in, we closed the door behind us.

"Before we get any further, I'm shifting into my other form, that way if we run into anyone, they won't question my being here, I'll tell them I brought you as a friend with me." Skylar started shifting into the other form as she spoke.

If she had a twin brother, he would have been attractive also, it looked strange to see a man standing there instead of Skylar. At least it would be easier to get used to her new look, something neither Micheal or Gregory had seen before.

"When we get back, I want to see how Gregory reacts to you in this form." Micheal laughed while pulling out a flashlight.

"What did you not bring with you?" Skylar looked surprised.

"This isn't the first place I've investigated. I like exploring abandoned homes, estates, caves and mining shafts so I stock most of my stuff back at the house." Micheal sounded proud of himself.

Flashing the light around, the room was rather large with an elevator at the far end. On one side there were metal bars from the ceiling to the floor with people standing behind it, not moving or showing any expressions. Next to them was a large shallow pool of an orangey green water. It was shallow enough to see the bottom. In the middle of the room, there was a large stone circle with a black sponge foam floor. Above it was a metal object and round ball at the end, it was connected to a large control panel in a half circular booth. A closer look at the people standing there, they were copies of Skylar and Gregory, none spoke and neither did they look at us as we flashed them with a light, except two who were fully exposed to the light exploded into ash. Careful not to take them all out, Micheal lowered the light. Noise started to come from the elevator as it came to the lowest floor. Micheal and Skylar made their way over to the filing cabinets and kneeled to watch from behind them. Akuma, Eisheth and several members from the order followed behind, all dressed in their silver and black robes.

Torches along the walls sprung to life as they glowed and lit up the side of the room the others were in. We could no longer see the stone circle as everyone stood around it. The cage opened and only one person came out when called. They didn't seem to care if they were trapped behind metal bars or not. One person stood over by the control booth, pushing a few buttons until there was a blue electrical bolt from the metal ball shooting down onto the person standing in the middle.

"Are you sure you wish to perform this on another duplicate; we could have more beneficial results if we used a fresh person." One of the hooded people spoke, at least we knew that one wasn't a water person.

"We could always use you if you wish to volunteer." Akuma

taunted the person.

"I'm sure you know what you're doing." Giving a slight bow, the person stood still.

They watched as the replica of Skylar stood on the foam pad, the electrical surge shot out and through the person exploding them. Not hiding her range, Akuma screamed while Eisheth stood there motionless, both Skylar and Micheal looked at each other wondering if Eisheth was a fake also but how could she last this long, was it the reason they said she was missing?

With her anger, she grabbed one of the robed figures and pushed them onto the foam mat, pulling the robe off the person so they were standing there naked, the person in the control booth pushed a few more buttons. The bolt of electricity shot through, shocking the person. The person trembled for a few seconds before dropping to the floor. There was a surge that ran along the floor over to the pool of ugly water and for a brief second the water creatures formed and then dropped back into the water.

Akuma grabbed her sister Eisheth pushing her onto the foam pad and again the control booth operator pushed buttons, and the electrical shot went through hitting her, she stood still shaking slightly but not reacting as the other had. Still standing after it was done, no one bothered to see if she was alright or if the person previously on the floor was alive. They were all looking over at the pool and watched the figures come to life as they fully formed from their feet upward and started being pushed from the pool as more was being made behind them. There was a total of forty replicas of Eisheth.

"Do you wish for us to send these where the others went?" One of the other robed people asked.

"No, their order has been fulfilled, these can last but still won't be able to talk, they can do as they are ordered but are still limited, we can't send them to any military bases yet, once we can get past this glitch, we will make so much more selling them. For now, fill some of the smaller orders." Akuma told them.

Observing the difference between the ones being kept behind the bars and those made from her sister, the ones behind the bars burst with artificial light and stood still like zombies. The others, even when told to follow, moved more naturally however still had a blank expression on their faces.

Akuma grabbed her sister by the arm pretty much dragging her over to the elevator, her sister was starting to drool a little.

"I don't think she's handling these very well." The robed person sounded concerned.

"She'll handle it until I say so, I can't risk testing it on myself and no one else has the ability to replicate like she does, has anyone found Gregory?" She looked at the others behind her.

"We haven't found him or the girl that was with him, his brother Micheal has gone missing, so we are guessing they are hiding somewhere in town, we searched their homes, Micheal's place was easy, we bribed Skylar's dog with food. There's a dog at Gregory's place that was easy to bribe but whatever the other furball was, we couldn't get in the house, it moved around so fast, the person searching was bleeding when they left but either way, no one was there either. I'm sure we will find them." The person tried to reassure her as the elevator door closed. The remaining people walked through the door in the corner.

Moving out from our area, Skylar took a few pictures with her cell phone of the control booth and the area the others were shot with electric and the pool. Skylar walked near the person who was laying on the ground, she hadn't recognized who the member was, but then the members she knew when she was a part of the order, she hadn't seen yet. Checking for a pulse, there wasn't one. Akuma was willing to sacrifice a person to get fake people made, she was already sacrificing her sister who she obviously didn't care for her safety or what she was doing to her.

While Skylar was checking on the person on the floor, I opened a few of the filing cabinet, there were so many files, each had a different name on it, checking through, I pulled the whole folder that either had Micheal, Skylar or Gregory listed on it. I also found the folders that listed Skylar's parents Joseph, Hazel and sister Carly along with Cora and Lewis, our parents. Slipping those and a few other files into the backpack, Sylar made her way back over ready to leave.

We walked back to the door we came in from before when we realized one of the duplicates from Eisheth was standing there. Tapping her on the shoulder, she turned and looked at us with no expression. We opened the door, and she followed behind us and she even closed the door behind us.

"Do we want to risk taking her with us in case they can figure out where we are staying?" Skylar was concerned.

"I think if they could do that, they would have noticed us right away, she was the first to wander away and they didn't pay attention. Probably when they were getting pushed out of the pool she was pushed too far over this way, and when told to follow, she went to the first door she saw. If she's able to follow us, then maybe we can see what these things can do." Micheal looked it over curious if it would be able to climb.

We made our way over to the rope and Skylar was the first one to climb up, Micheal was waiting for the clone to follow, hoping this might work, Micheal told her to follow Skylar. Once he said this, she started to climb the rope quickly and stood next to Skylar once she was at the top. Looking around, we hadn't seen anyone, so we made our way back to the cabin. We knew Greogry had to be driving himself crazy waiting not knowing how we were doing. There wasn't much to search for and thankfully it hadn't taken us very long.

Micheal went into the cabin first to prepare Gregory even though he hadn't expected to see him holding a broom handle as if he expected to fence him with it.

"Are you intending to fight off the enemy with that broom stick?" Micheal laughed.

"Where is Skylar, is she safe?" I looked around him trying to see if she was going to be coming through the door.

"Yes, she is fine, but we have a surprise, don't attack who is coming in." Micheal said without giving away too much.

"Do you remember what educational degrees our parents had?" I was wondering if they were trained to handle the equipment downstairs.

"Both mom and dad had a bachelor's degree in chemical engineering. Dad worked as a university instructor for a couple of years." Micheal said as he sat down on the couch.

"Is it alright to come in?" Skylar asked from outside.

"Yeah, he's going to freak out." Micheal laughed.

Skylar walked in and I took a step back without thinking about it, I was expecting to see Skylar except there was a man standing there with wide shoulders, wavy dark brown hair, he looked like a brother of hers not that she had one, she did have a sister. Then the woman behind him shocked me the most.

"This technically is Akuma's sister Eisheth but she's a duplicate, we watched the process being done, they are using people but not everyone has the ability to. They seem to be positive you would be better than her sister. We brought this one back with us to see what it can do. So far, it can climb a rope with no problems." Skylar stated.

"It sounds strange hearing your voice and seeing you in the body of a man. Thank you for not morphing into something while we were intimate earlier." I was feeling creeped out.

"Micheal thought you might like to see what I can change into; I can copy many others and if Akuma knew that, she would be searching for me as much as you." Skylar stated as she slowly changed back.

"You still have stubble." Micheal stated.

"One of the draw backs, I can change everything back except there is sometimes a little hair on my face or other places where it doesn't belong." Skylar sounded disappointed.

She left us there with the clone while she went to get rid of the excess body hair.

"I'm surprised she's risking her sister to make one of these." I looked her over as she looked at me which made me feel creepy.

"She seems to like you. We are positive that Akuma has pretty much killed her sister, at least she's not there mentally and struggles existing, she's just dragging her along now." Micheal stated as he started pulling folders out.

Opening the one with Gregory on it, Micheal first saw several photos of his brother tied up and what looked like either Akuma or Eiseth having sex with him, then there were several of the others doing the same. There were several sheets with his medical information such as allergies, blood type and all observations they'd made about him since he was twelve, all very short and to the point, his folder was thicker than anyone else. Micheal handed it to me, and I blushed as I saw there were photos.

"I don't want to explain these." I felt embarrassed and hoped no one else saw these.

"How many times did you meet with the mystery person?" Micheal asked.

"Honestly, twice and both times it involved sex, they used condoms, at least they felt like condoms thankfully." I wasn't sure what else to say.

"There is a page with the results of what they collected from those condoms, interesting. My own file here has a lot of information I didn't know about myself but it's not as thick as yours, I'm listed as 'an average person of no use' so no more information was apparently needed on me. I do wonder if we had sex with the same person, it describes my sexual encounter with Akuma. She came to my house, didn't announce herself and all she did was strip down naked in front of me and we had sex on the couch. Afterward I was going to ask her a question, she put her finger to my lip to stop me from talking and then she left carrying her clothes with her." Micheal was about to look through Skylar's folder when I snatched it away from him.

"She might not like you seeing this." I spoke.

"What might I not want you to see. You've both seen me nude.

Hasn't anyone told her to sit down?" Skylar asked, walking back into the room.

"Eisheth, sit down on the chair while we read through the folders." Micheal stated.

The clone walked over to the nearest chair and sat down still not talking with no expression.

"Can she smile?" I wondered as I handed Skylar her folder.

Eisheth, can you smile?" Skylar asked her.

The clone attempted to smile but it not only looked creepy but very evil and nothing like a genuine smile, a true human would have used the muscle around their eyes, cheeks and lips, not just the lips themselves. No wonder they are expressionless.

"They got some great shots of my butt," Skylar pulled out a picture and showed both of us, "I'm guessing they took pictures of all of us nude. There are a few older ones when I tried getting into the order before I started to shift into a male."

"They liked Gregory, he has the most, but he also met up with them more often than he told us. When did they snag you Skylar?" Micheal asked.

"I was suntanning on the beach when a stranger started to massage suntan lotion on me and before I knew it, we were having sex. The first time was when I willingly went in for an orgy with the group, but they turned me down. They never complained when I was a male." Skylar smiled wistfully.

"I'm going into town to grab more items that we need. I have a feeling they are going to get more desperate looking for you and I think the best place to stay is here and I don't want either of you going into town and being seen anymore. I'll be back soon." Micheal said as he emptied the backpack except, he kept a few things in it and left us there with the clone.

Not that we knew what we were going to do with her, but we also had several folders to read through.

# Chapter Twelve

Before reading the files, Skylar found an outfit for the clone to wear. It took a while to read through all the folders, Skylar had fun going through mine, watching me blush as she looked at the pictures. We found after reading the ones with our parents' names on them, that they started the project but it wasn't supposed to go beyond temporary, the water creatures were supposed to be easy to create anywhere by anyone and would last until artificial light was on it, then it was supposed to decompose into a powder, the light dried up whatever water was left in it and the other chemicals would end up dropping into a powder. It was interesting, it had to be artificial and not natural light.

Akuma wanted to make them more permanent and wanted them for more uses than sex toys. She wanted them as realistic as possible, to either replace real people, used for military purposes, there were so many uses listed. It would have been fine but the fact she had a long list of people she killed to control the entire thing and not share it with anyone. It listed a vault where she kept the DNA of those she killed, so she could reconstruct them when she could make it permanent, and her sisters name was there also.

"If you ever want to put me in the mood, just show me these pictures." Skylar smiled as she flashed them at me again.

I tried to grab it from her, but Skylar pulled it away before I could. We had been sitting here for quite a while and the clone hadn't looked anywhere else or moved. It felt strange having it there.

"Eisheth, can you speak?" I was curious if she was able to.

She looked up at me but hadn't spoken, her mouth didn't move but she knew I was the one talking to her.

"Eisheth, can you clean the dishes?" Skylar asked her for an action.

Standing up, she went over to the right side where there was a small countertop with a sink. She found a cloth and placed it on the counter and then put the holder from under the sink, on top of the counter. Grabbing a sponge, soap and running the water, she started to wash the dishes and place them in the holder to air dry. Once she was done, she stood there motionless. We decided to see what else she could do, having her follow us down to the fourth floor, we had her walk on the treadmill. After thirty minutes we stopped, she wasn't exhausted or breathing heavily so we were sure her lungs were not developed, or she didn't have any.

While Skylar had her doing various exercises, I looked through the science room looking for anything we could to see the inside of her. There was a small portable one, I assumed this was one of the last items added to the room. I began to wonder if our parents started to work here or kept their work safe here because the others didn't know it was here. Pulling the screen on a cart, I brought it downstairs, I didn't want her going inside the lab.

We had her lay down on the mat as we placed a board under her back and fit the machine over her. Taking the picture, we both looked at each other wondering the same thing.

"I knew my parents had money, but they must have been loaded to buy all of this. I've been to this place countless times, but the doors were always sealed, I had no interest in checking them out, I wonder what unsealed them?" Skylar looked confused.

"I was going to ask you if you knew anything about this but now, I don't need to." I pulled the machine back once it started to show.

Micheal returned while we were waiting on the picture to fully process. Watching it felt like it took ages, but we were anxious. It looked like she had a basic skeletal system but no nerve endings anywhere. We did the same with her head, where the brain should be, instead of a normal one resembling a large, shriveled walnut. In the center part of her brain, there was a tiny metal square. She had basically everything a normal human would have, heart, lungs, kidney, spleen, bladder that a normal human would need to survive except the central nervous system. We couldn't figure out how she was processing thoughts without it.

"Will you stop ex-raying your penis. It might sterilize you." I couldn't believe Micheal was playing with the x-ray machine.

"That's okay, I wasn't planning on having kids. Seriously, look at me, do you think I should raise kids?" Micheal laughed as he said it.

As I put the machine back in its room, Skylar kept giving her directions, watching to see how quickly she started or realized she was finished with the task. She looked and felt like a real human being, but she was missing the soul of one, how did they think replicating Gregory through the machine would result in better options than they were already able to produce.

"I partly want to go back to our town and see if I can get close to any of the followers and find out more information from them. We can't hide forever and yes, we have enough evidence to show them to arrest her, but if she finds out she might take off." Micheal stated.

"What are we going to do with her?" Skylar asked.

"Keep the place clean?" Micheal looked confused.

"What if they have more replicas of us out there, the pit was deep and there were a lot of them that formed, and I didn't see any mounds of dust unless it was blown away or they removed it. We already saw them move a few of our replicas to another room for, as Akuma said, a smaller order. There were a lot more than that so where did the others go?" Skylar hated the idea of people thinking those fakes were them.

"Maybe I should give them what they want, I could show up and have them take me, keep the tracker on me so you can find me even though we know where we are going to end up, and maybe I can ruin it making them think there is no further way of improving the water creatures." It wasn't the best idea, but it was a start.

"And if they find there is no need of you, they might kill you off like they did our parents." Skylar stopped talking when we heard a sound from outside.

We were careful not to go near the windows even though they were grimy, and you couldn't see through them well, with the black out curtains no one would be able to see. Skylar closed her eyes focusing on an image and her body started to change. Looking in the mirror she was happy with her image, she looked like an old woman. That's when I noticed Micheal change his image to match her as an elderly gentleman.

"Once we can, both of you need to teach me how to do that. I'll take the clone to the bedroom so I can listen in case you need me." Telling the clone to follow, we went into the first room, and I kept the door closed.

I knew I could hear better with the door open, but I didn't want to risk the clone walking out if she thought she was being given a command. Both Skylar and Micheal stood near the front door in their new shapes, opening the door slowly as if they were truly elderly, they looked out first and no one was standing there, not wanting to get jumped, Skylar disguised her voice and spoke out loud.

"Hello, please don't make an old lady come look for you." She said hoping the person would let their guard down.

85

There wasn't anyone speaking but they could hear more knocking, Micheal took a slight look outside and could see a person knocking on trees. Feeling confused as to why she would be out there looking lost and expressionless.

"Do you think that is her or Akuma faking it hoping to draw us out?" Skylar asked.

"I'm not sure, I don't like the idea of giving away our hiding spot but if it's her sister, I think she's too far gone to give away any information. If anything, she needs medical help." Micheal stated.

"My parents have their old jeep out back, it probably needs a jump, but we could use that to bring her in, I don't think you should go alone, last thing we need is them thinking you did this to her. We can go in our disguise, no one would assume anything from a couple of old people." Skylar looked around outside before collecting the real Eisheth and bringing her inside.

"I'll go work on the jeep and get it ready and I'll call for you." Micheal went out through the farthest back and into the garage.

We could hear him tinkering around, I opened the door assuming the clone would be safe in there. I didn't give her any commands, but she followed me out.

"Do you think this is a set up or do you think she's really out of it?" I noticed she was slightly drooling.

"The last action her sister did, caused this to her. We need to be careful how we drop her off, if they start searching in our area, they will assume we harmed her because of all the lab equipment but if we could direct them to the actual place they could investigate it, but unfortunately Akuma might set up somewhere else." Skylar sounded worried.

As we waited for the jeep to get started. Skylar grabbed a soft cloth and wiped the corner of Eisheth's mouth. Micheal called her and they both brought the real person with them to the jeep, another time I was going to worry about them being gone. They were going to tell the hospital they dropped her off at, that they found her wandering along the main road knocking on trees. Once she was safely collected by them, they would make their way back here. Until then I would fill in time again.

This time when I watched them leave, I made sure all the curtains were closed, and the doors were locked with the security alarm on. I kept feeling like the others wouldn't let her wonder unless they were not worried since she couldn't speak and maybe her brain was already far too damaged. I noticed the clone followed me everywhere without having to say something.

"I never gave you another command after we went to the bedroom." I was curious why she was still following me.

I wasn't exactly expecting a response from her, so I went back out to the couch and sat down. The clone followed me and sat down on the couch. She continued to look forward and I looked around her. Trying to find anything. I knew it would show up in the x-ray, but nothing was there unless the metal box in her brain was something. Watching her I kept looking for any twitch.

"Are you a robot?" I hoped she might be able to say something.

"I respond to master only." She said while looking forward.

"You mean you only speak to the master; Skylar gave you directions and you followed them." It felt strange hearing her speak.

"Actions are anyone, speaking to master only." She spoke.

"What makes me the master." I asked.

"Akuma stated Gregory is master." She spoke.

"And I'm Gregory?" I wondered how she knew since none of us addressed each other in front of her.

"It's stored in my brain. I have a file containing all the information about you." She spoke.

"How do you function without a nervous system?" I wanted to know more about her.

"I have clear fiber optics that carry to each of the areas its needed. I am constantly charged if I am around you, I only function on backup when I am not." She stated.

"Do you know who has had sex with me?" I was curious if she would know personal information.

"First was Akuma, I have and clones three, five, seven, twelve, fourteen and sixteen." She stated.

"Are those the only clones?" It seems strange I wouldn't know the difference between a real person and fake one.

"Clones are stored until they are required. Most do not last long, those who service are from my original." She stated again.

"Where are the clones kept?" I knew neither Skylar or Micheal said they saw a group of clones other than the small group behind the bars.

"They are in the old wood mill. "She said.

I knew where the wood mill was located, and it wasn't far from here. I wanted to see what clones they had. I hoped both Micheal and Skylar would get back soon so we could check it out. I didn't like the idea of others making out with a clone of me or someone thinking I was going to war when it wasn't me. If they were more creative and made their own looks it would be fine, but I wasn't happy with someone duplicating me without my permission.

"Why did Akuma name me master." I was curious.

"She needs you to make things work." She said.

"If things work when I'm around, if they are sold then they won't work away from me, how could I possibly help." I felt confused.

"Your DNA would be added to each one, they will only stop when destroyed." She said.

"How can Akuma be stopped?" I was curious how truthful the clone would be.

"She can't. The plan is laid out." She said.

"What if I were put in the cloning machine." I asked.

"It would scramble DNA making you useless as the original Eisheth." She stated.

"Did Eisheth choose to be cloned?" I asked.

"It was done for the greater good, master Akuma decided." She stated.

"Do you obey her or me?" I asked.

"I obey Gregory first to preserve." She stated.

I wasn't sure what to think of it. The door in the back closed when I realized they were back. I swear I could easily be walked in on without knowing. Once they were near me, they looked at me curiously and I knew they must have heard another voice.

"Who were you talking to?" Micheal asked as he looked strangely at the clone.

"That would be the clone, apparently, she can answer me because Akuma has it stored in the metal box that I am the master and to be obeyed first to be preserved. I got a few answers out of her, at least now I have a better understanding of how she can operate, but she isn't programmed to respond to anyone else. How did they respond when you dropped the original off?" I wondered if they had any problems.

"They thanked us thinking we were wonderful for being brave and grabbing her when we didn't know who she was or if she was a drug user possibly having an episode from it. They took her in right away, not that they could share how she was doing since its personal medical information, but they said they would do their best to find out who she was." We simply told her an area we found her when we were driving to the next town to go home. We had to give a little more information, so we said we were going home from visiting our older sister and her husband." Micheal smiled and I could guess it was him who came up with it.

"At least we got rid of one, but what are we going to do with this one?"

Skylar asked.

"This clone told me where the other clones were being kept. I wanted to check it out. I don't want to risk bringing her with us, we can leave her in the bedroom, she's not strong enough to escape." I figured in there she would be safe.

"The padded room would be better; she can't get hurt or move a curtain if someone is outside." Skylar said as she was looked the clone over.

Without saying a word, the clone started to follow me. I made it to the second floor where the sex room was, there was a small, padded room off to the side, I still hadn't investigated it other than there were no other ways out. At least she didn't need anything, so we left her in there. At first, she did try to follow me out once I stepped out of the room, but she could not operate the door.

# Chapter Thirteen

We all got into the jeep and started to drive towards the old mill, it felt strange seeing Skylar look old, neither remembered to change not that they needed to, it was probably a better idea they stayed in this form, I just wish I could do the same. I tried concentrating on another face but all I could do was develop a headache, then I heard Skylar laughing.

"You're trying to change form? It takes a lot of practice; at the beginning you will get a lot of headaches. I'll teach you a little when we get back." She said as she turned to look out the window.

We drove for a little while down a winding narrow two track dirt road. There were no lights out here, so it was extremely dark. We could slightly see part of a wood building coming into view. When we were closer, there was an old wheel half fallen off into the water that used to turn it. The glass was broken with several boards missing. If they wanted it to look like no one was here in years, then they won that award, but it could also be a trap, my brain was running, overly thinking this could be a trick to trap us. If it was, I didn't want to risk their lives since I was the one who insisted on doing this. Parking near the building, Micheal took out three flashlights and handed us each one. Turning them on, we followed the path to the front door. It had a brand-new shiny padlock. Instead, Skylar went over to one of the windows and carefully pulled out the small piece of windowpane, setting it on the ground. Then balanced herself getting inside. We both followed her. There wasn't anything on the first floor, we looked around on the second floor and hadn't found anything either.

"I don't understand it, she said the old mill, this is the only one I know of that's close by and closed." I was confused.

"Do you think she lied to you and maybe has a beacon on her so the others can track her, not that they knew we were there to take her with us." Skylar said.

"I don't know I keep feeling like we are missing something." I felt there had to be more to it.

"You mean like this little hatch on the side of the building?" Micheal pointed at standing next to the window.

Looking out the window at it, that was it. Making our way back out the window and around to the side, we walked watching the ground for any traps not that we found any. They must have been incredibly confidant no one would check out here. There were no locks, but the lid took all three of us to lift. Leaving it open, we went down the stairs and flashed our lights ahead. We didn't have to go far before we ran into the clones, they were all standing there packed in like sardines. I looked over at Skylar and asked her if she was alright, she looked sad as she looked at a particular clone.

"I knew them, the three over in the corner. They were good friends, they looked lost like the original Eisheth, their clones are right next to them. If I had stayed any longer, they might have tried it with me and found out what I was able to do and destroyed me the way Akuma did with her sister." Skyler made her way over to them, giving each of her friends a hug.

"Our clones are in the back room; this place is huge, and it goes under the sawmill. There's five of each. I have an odd question for you, if I have my clone suck my dick, is that the same as incest?" Micheal asked with a smile.

"No, but that's gross. These people are not entirely real, and not us but they are something, just don't do it, if you must ask, don't." I knew Micheal was always horny.

"I wonder how many of these would turn to dust if they were in direct sunlight?" Skylar asked.

"They get plenty of light, there are a few holes up there but no lightbulbs to accidentally destroy them." Micheal pointed out a few of the holes above.

"We could always steal ours and four more, but I know realistically we can't hide all of them." Skylar was looking at both me and Micheal.

"We could have our own private sex parties." Micheal tried to sound cheerful.

"Again, just no. it's already going to be difficult dropping off three more people, once this happens, they are going to know something is up and will start investigating it. We need to drop them off at a further town over, they need medical help, but I don't know if they have a chance again, If we left them here they would never be taken care of, at least with the medical community they will be properly cared for. We could lead the police to this location, its away from our place but if they see clones of us and find out we are missing, it will get them looking for us." I wasn't sure what to do with all of them.

I noticed I started to get a group following me around. I assumed it was for the same reason as the girl back at the cabin. I walked over to the far side of the room as Micheal and Skylar gave orders to the others to go up the stairs, thankfully they listened to them. I made my way up and before the others could get out, we replaced the door. We made our way back to the cabin much slower this time, we could not fit everyone in the vehicle, so we went extremely slow with me walking behind otherwise they stopped and would not continue walking.

Once we were at the cabin, we locked the others in the padded room also, then the three originals we kept in the vehicle, we drove over to the main highway and went down a distance, we all felt strange not doing this with the small town department but we had a feeling if Akuma wasn't afraid of being caught, she might have already done something to them. We could see bright lights in the distance, and we knew we were at the nearest city.

Skylar walked into the police department and set a note at the desk of a gentleman who told her he would be with her in a moment, once he looked up, she was already gone but he picked up her note. It said, people will continue to be found and dropped off at hospitals, but they might not be normal again. There are people trapped in a room and you can't leave it to the local department to handle it, whatever you do, don't go alone and don't trust Akuma.

Then we drove to a hospital in the area and went up to the emergency department, helping the three get out, Skylar felt bad for leaving them but there wasn't anything we could do for them. They stood there as we took off and the staff came out with a security guard looking confused thinking we might be parking until they saw us drive away.

When we made it back to the cabin, we locked the vehicle in the garage and sat down in the living room. Skylar pulled out her laptop and used the signal from her phone to access the internet. Checking the local news. There was a report on the first girl that was found, they were calling her Jane Doe, they said they had a person claim her at first saying it was her sister and we were worried Akuma was going to try and collect her again except she backed out now that they know about the other three.

They were asking for any information known about these

people, they were testing their blood to help identify them soon. Their condition was being discussed heavily and they were worried about a cult, we guessed it would be the right word for now.

"If no one needs me, mind if go play cards with the clones?" Micheal said as he stood up.

"You don't play cards." Skylar challenged him.

"Fine, can I go have sex with one of them?" He stated firmly.

"You have the real thing here and you prefer a clone?" Skylar joked with him.

"Gregory claimed dibs on you years ago, not that it ever stopped things, but yeah, I'll settle for a duplicate." Micheal smiled as he went down to the second floor.

"What did he mean it didn't stop things?" I asked.

"Since you were so definite about not dating or getting physical with me, I experimented with Micheal. I did it to make you jealous, but nothing seemed to work, I guess it's why I was surprised you were willing to when I was tied and expecting someone else." Skylar didn't want to discuss it.

"My premonitions might not be understood a hundred percent but out of eleven people I've seen die, it came true for ten of them, it's one of the reasons it scared me about you, I didn't want to risk losing you." I still had the thought at the back of my mind that she might.

I'm going to bug Micheal while he's trying to have sex. I swear, if I had him around more often, I probably would be horny more often, he has that way of rubbing off on you. Even at the most inappropriate times." Skylar smiled as she walked out of the room.

I didn't want to watch my brother make out with anyone and I was worried if I went in there, I would have all the clones staring at me. When I went by the padded room, I could look in through the glass, Micheal was enjoying one and after counting I could see Skylar took one to her bedroom. I looked in Skylar's room carefully to see she hadn't picked one of my clones. I went back to the padded room, looked around for her and found Eisheth and brought her into another bedroom with me. Sitting her on the bed next to me, I thought maybe I would try to talk with her.

"I know I asked this before, but when I had sex in the cave, did anyone else, meaning nonclone have sex with me other than Akuma?" I asked the clone.

"No, she ordered no one else touch you until she did." She stated.

"Do you have a name? It feels strange calling you by the originals name." It felt strange after what happened and I felt strange almost disrespectful using that name with her.

"I have no other name then clone two." She stated again.

"Do you want your own name?" I asked.

"Want?" She asked.

"Yes, want, when people want something. Micheal and I didn't always share well when we were kids, so if I wanted my own car and he wanted it, we both would get one. Or when we had friends, they were usually our own friends, it wasn't often we both shared the same friend. Or when we want sex, it's getting our wants and desires, a house falling apart wants to be fixed. I might not be the right person to describe this."

She sat there for a few minutes not saying anything. I was positive it was pointless trying to get her to pick out a name, I wasn't sure if I could rename her since she was a clone and how the box in her head worked would affect it. She turned her head to look at me and started to speak.

"Is Nova acceptable." She asked.

"You want to be called Nova? That is perfectly fine. I am curious how you picked that name." I was surprised she was able to give it thought.

"Your obsessed with science, something you learned from your parents, but they were earth bound, you prefer the skies. A super nova star exploding is brilliant and something you would like so I chose Nova." She said.

"That's excellent reasoning. Congratulations." I said to her.

She sat there with a blank stare, and I hadn't wanted to explain another word right now.

"It's okay, we can work on what compliments are later." I kept staring at her instead of moving

It was easier when the other person took advantage of me or when Skylar wasn't expecting it. This wasn't a person who would turn me down but even still I had a difficult time knowing how to start now that I knew she might not feel it, I wasn't sure how Micheal was able to do this with no problem or Skylar for that matter.

I ran my hand up her leg and it felt like a woman's leg. Standing up off the bed, I stood in front of her, taking the lower part of her shirt and pulling it up over her head. Putting it on the nightstand, I put my hands on her breasts and rubbed my hands over them, cupping and massaging them. I guess for me I was hoping for a reaction. I told her to lay back on the bed and she did. I rubbed my hand between her legs, fingered her labia a little and slowly stuck a finger in. Pulling my finger out and keeping my hand in an L shape, I put all four fingers in and a little further.

"Do you feel my fingers in you?" I asked.

"I sense where they are." She said.

"Are you really asking her if she feels anything? I get you like to be connected but she's never going to feel or be a real person. It's like an upgraded sex doll. If its sexy talk, you need a lot more practice." Skylar was standing there watching me for a moment.

"How long were you standing there?" I was sort of happy she came into the room.

"Let me do you a fun favor, later on we'll figure out what we are going to do with these things but for now, its learning their place." Skylar said as she had her person sit on the chair in the corner of the room.

"She chose a new name, instead of calling her clone, she's going to be called Nova." I was still impressed by the way she picked it.

"Maybe she will do better than the others because of who she is cloned after." Skylar said as she took Nova's hands and placed them over her own breasts.

"I wish she would talk when either you or Micheal talked to her instead of only me. The first time I heard her speak she sounded exactly like Eisheth but now that she's talked a few times, her voice is starting to sound a little different." I hoped I wasn't imagining it.

"I swear your like a kid, you're supposed to have sex, not explore her." Skylar laughed.

Skylar's clone wasn't wearing any clothes making it easier for her to grab his penis, she stroked it in front of me, making her point to play with them.

"That's your thing, I'm interested in sex and any other time I would be trying out things I was too nervous with a real person, but we don't know much about these clones, so I'm fascinated by how she works. When I was in the cave, I played along and it was exciting not knowing what was happening even though I should have been concerned, part of me just wanted to let go. But I couldn't help but feel connected to her, except I didn't know she wasn't real." While feeling her, there was no indication that she wasn't a normal human.

Skylar directed her person to lay on the other side of Nova. She kept playing with his penis holding it firmly in her hand. I was curious if he would speak with me the way Nova did.

"Can you speak?" I asked him.

"Yes." He said.

"Okay, you proved they will speak only to you, I wish they would talk to all of us or not at all, then we could teach them to have dirty bedroom talk."

Skylar sounded disappointed when she let go of his penis.

"Do you have a metal box in your head, and can you make changes to it?" I asked him again.

"I can receive updated software." He said.

"How do we update your software?" I asked him.

"Through the ear." He pointed to a tiny hole in the side of his ear.

"Do you have a way to connect to that?" I asked him.

"It's in the shirt pocket on the floor in the padded room." He said.

"Only you could ruin an easy lay." Skylar looked disappointed and got up leaving the room.

"They are great for that, but I think our parents saw them for more than that, if they truly take direction well and work great, they could be used for volunteer work." All the possibilities were running through my thoughts.

When she left, I went into the padded room searching through all the shirts, and I found every single one had one. Taking one and leaving, I realized what Micheal was doing, guessing his goal was to have sex with all the clones in the room, it wasn't going to be fun cleaning them up afterward. Once I got the cord, I brought the two out into the living room and connected them to the laptop. There were so many files and making a few modifications inside, I hoped to see what they would do, while they were loading, I gave them the instructions to stay put until I came back.

# Chapter Fourteen

Once I had everything set, I went to find Skylar, I knew I wasn't exactly acting the way she wanted but I was obsessed over the new clones. She wasn't in her room or the padded room, she wasn't in the living room, so I went into the room with all the adult toys. She was over on the mat with one of the clones and this time it was my clone. I stood at the door watching her, she had the dildo on, not the one she used on me, it was the much thicker one, I could see what I would have looked like if she used it on me and I must admit, it would hurt. It's a good thing the clones don't have pain receptors.

She was pounding into him rather hard, occasionally leaning forward to add more pressure. She was taking her frustration out on him that she meant for me.

"Does it hurt? Of course it does, not that you will ever know. Your ass feels just like his, but I won't get the same moaning out of you. I know he doesn't like it, unlike him, you will like it." As she kept thrusting the dildo in roughly.

"Sorry to interrupt, but I am reprogramming the one in the living room so he will respond to you. I can do the same with this one so when your mad at me, it will seem more realistic." I felt bad because I was frustrating her.

Turning to look at me, "I was turned on when I saw you playing with her and then you completely missed the mark. I don't know if I should keep expecting something from you or accept the fact that we will always be just friends, either way I wish I knew so I could train my mind not to see you in a certain way. Do I need to be tied up and blindfolded every time for you to have sex with me?" Skylar asked.

"No, you don't, even though you are sexy tied up. Instead of you taking your frustrations out on him, you can give me any order you want, and I'll do it or have done to me. I am yours to control. I can't promise I won't make mistakes in the future, I get distracted and obsessed about things, but I've never been great at initiating things around you, Whenever I'm in your presence, an overwhelming wave of nervousness washes over me, as if the very air around us crackles with electricity. I've lost count of how many nights I've dreamt of you, each vision a vivid tapestry woven from threads of admiration and yearning. To me, you are not just an ephemeral figure; you embody my ultimate goddess and the essence of my deepest desires. Yet, standing beside you reveals my insecurities—I can't help but feel inadequate and imperfect in contrast to the perfection I see before me. Your beauty and grace leave me awestruck, igniting within me both admiration and a profound sense of vulnerability that echoes long after we part ways. I feel too awkward around you, anyone else is easy, but they are not you." I knew it wouldn't fix missing what she wanted before, but it was a start.

"It would help knowing I'm putting you in pain for frustrating me." Skylar smiled.

She pulled the dildo out from the clone, leaving him to lay there, pointing out where she wanted me. I regretted my words, but I knew I made a promise. Getting down on all fours, I stayed there waiting for her while she dripped oil over me, massaging it in and to try and insert the dildo. I could feel the pressure from it all the way around my anus. This wasn't something I was going to be recovering from right away and would be sore.

"I promise once this is in, it will be sliding in and out slowly since it was almost impossible to move when it was in the clone." She said.

"I know, it looked like you were struggling but he also was having a difficult time not being pulled back with it." It was not something I was looking forward to.

She pressed the Dildo against the rim a few more times, once I felt the pinch and flinched slightly before she started laughing.

"What's so funny?" I wasn't sure what she was thinking.

"You have no idea how hard it was getting this thing into him, I'm pretty sure since you tighten up, I might never get it into you but the fact you would let me do anything to you. Come hug me." Skylar said.

Turning over to a sitting position I leaned forward wrapping my arms around Skylar pulling her onto my lap, brushing my lips over her soft lips, I kissed her softly at first, but my entire body ached for her. Kissing her firmer on the lips, feeling I was completely taken over by her. Laying back, I helped her turn until her legs were on either side of me, she leaned over continuing to kiss me. Sliding her forward slightly I was going to have her ride me. She sat up and slowly went down on me, now moving her hips around slightly in a circular motion. Placing my hands on either side of her hips, I loved feeling her move.

"You are incredibly sexy." I moaned as she started to move quicker.

"I like how you moan when I move faster." Skylar said." I said.

"I love the way you feel in me, especially when I can do deeper." Skylar started to grind faster.

"I love when you plunge down hard on me. I love it rough." As I whispered it.

"You said anything I want." Skylar gave me a mischievous smile.

"Yes, I said anything you want. Any fantasy or whatever turns you on, both clones are watching rather intently." I was surprised to see both sitting up watching us.

"You probably shouldn't have said that." Skylar smiled.

Skylar reached over grabbing one of the golf size vibrating balls with a string on it, she had already used it on the clone, sliding back between my legs, she had me roll back over on all fours as she worked its way into my anus. I should learn to limit when I say anything. She layered it with oil, there was a small tip at the end of the ball, no doubt to help it start going in, it took several tries as she slowly pushed the ball in so the only thing showing was the string to pull it back out. I wasn't sure exactly what she had on her mind yet, but it felt strange having it start to vibrate, she had a small little clicker the size of her thumb that could change the settings. Laying on her back, she motioned for me to climb up over her and she grabbed my penis with her hand.

"I want you to slide slowly into me." Skylar asked.

As I lowered myself, I slid between her legs and into her vagina. She kept smiling at me and I knew this wouldn't be it, but now all I could feel was the strong vibration from the ball.

"Tell your clone to place his penis in your anus." Skylar asked.

"Clone that is laying on the floor, come behind me and put your penis in my anus." It felt strange trying to figure out how to direct him.

The clone stood up and walked over behind me, kneeled and placed his penis by my anus. So far, I was used to things being inserted carefully except I hadn't specified for him to be careful not that I was sure he would know what that was. Shoving hard, I felt the pinch and shoved forward as he forced himself in me. I could feel a slight burning sensation, he hit the ball as it continued to vibrate.

"You'll have to give him more instructions than to put his penis in you otherwise he will just kneel there with it in you. Did he put it all the way?" Skylar asked.

"Yes, he did. I wasn't ready for it but it's in there. Give me a moment to think how to word this." I had to take a second to think.

"Tell him to pull out halfway and slam back into you repeatedly until you say stop." Skylar said as she placed motioned for me to pull my knees closer to my chest but still on either side of Skylar so that it caused my ass to be more up in the air.

She grabbed by buttocks and slid her hand to my anus to feel him in me.

"Are you sure?" I gave her a chance to change her mind.

"Yes, I'm sure." She said.

"Clone, pull your penis out halfway and slam back into me repeatedly until I say stop." I did say I would do anything for her.

I didn't want to admit it was turning me on knowing this excited her. I loved the way she felt me as this was happening. The clone started to thrust into me fast, pushing me forward slightly as he slammed into me, he hadn't held back at all, and Skylar kept feeling his penis with her hand as he entered me every time. Once he was in and moving back and forth, I was surprised by the sensation, it only hurt when he first entered but now it felt unusually good.

"How does he feel in you?" Skylar asked me.

"It's like entering a woman but the muscle glands are much tighter. It feels incredibly good." It was difficult talking, I laid more on Skylar turning my head to the side as he thrust hard into me.

Honestly, I hadn't wanted it to end. Skylar was getting turned on and it felt good as she fingered around my anus as I was getting thrusted into. Unfortunately, certain people have the worst timing.

Micheal came in smirking as he watched us. We might have liked the fact the room had mirrors all the way around the room but there were times it would be nice for a little privacy but at this point we'd seen everything about each other.

I'm guessing you both have your phone alerts off but I got this a few minutes ago, officials are urging people to keep their doors locked, to be careful who they pick up on the road, there was a huge surge of originals being dropped off or found roadside and it's not only our four total, other towns found them and police are now seeing them. Apparently, they raided the hatch by the mill. All they said was a group of people who were being kept against their will and who were not physically or mentally well. I guess it's safer than saying they are clones, that and they have a warrant for arrest for Akuma. They've had news about it nonstop. I'm glad we grabbed ours but Akuma no doubt is hearing the same news we are and must realize we took ours. I'm curious if she's hiding in the bunker, I don't see her wanting to stay in the cabin in our town since most of them would direct the police there. And one last thing, those clones out in the main room are having a conversation with each other." Micheal looked at me questioningly.

"It's okay, you can go. I'll get these cleaned up and I'll be out soon. I'm not touching the ones Micheal had with him, that's to gross, you are cleaning those yourself." Skylar said as she stood up.

Grabbing clothes and getting dressed, I walked up to the living room to see the two next to the laptop talking to each other as any normal human would. I used the flash drive that was in the journal left behind by my parents, I assumed it was one more piece that Akuma needed.

"Can you believe they are communicating with each other, none of the others are but these two and they are connected to a wire." Micheal looked at them in disbelief.

"I connected the wire and added more information into their system, conversational thought process. I know there is one more piece to add and it's also what Akuma is missing, I don't know if our parents ever figured it out but when I was first talking to Nova in the bedroom, I kept thinking maybe it's the ability to shift. When we can, or at least you and Skylar can, I have the ability to but haven't learned yet, maybe if they had that, they could fully function and be more human. It might never be fully functional and sustainable as a human but certainly closer to it. Maybe that's why Akuma thinks I would be able to give that to them. Strange since I've never shifted, and both of you have that she values me over them, there must be something else?" I still felt confused.

"I think I know what the key is, it's not shifting, it's the fact you have inscribed and absorbed into your body the very thing that kept you from dying several years ago, the ancient book of our ancestors. If a non-shifter or non-Fae did, they would have died." Skylar said as she joined us.

The television had been on mute however the banner across the bottom in red caught our attention, with Micheal turning it up, it had an urgent news report warning of possible danger. They were testing various lakes to make sure there wasn't a virus spreading. Also, there were several prominent figures missing with no warning where their location might be. Reports of missing people were being reported and warning people not to risk leaving their homes unless they are in a group or armed, the risk hadn't been assessed yet and no indicator to say what was causing the rash of kidnappings.

"Do you think she's still using the main place near here; I doubt she would use the hatch since they raided that already and we don't know of any other location she might be using, not that it doesn't mean there isn't one." Micheal said.

"I think she will continue to use this one, it didn't look temporary, we didn't see what was in the other room and the equipment was rather new and expensive. I don't see her ditching it quite yet." I said.

"I wouldn't mind checking it out again but if she's under the pressure she is now, it will be harder to get in, I'm surprised we haven't seen any activity around here yet." Micheal said.

"I have a day left before I go back to work; my place might be watched, especially since she knows my connection to you. I don't know if she's aware of where I work or if she's looking for me at all anymore, the main person is you, Gregory." Skylar said.

"I agree we should check the place out again, but we need to be prepared, she won't hand over the people she's taken willingly, not that I know how to stop her yet but I'm hoping we will figure it out." I said.

"I wonder what they did with the clones they picked up from the hatch they raided." Micheal asked.

"Before we go there, I can't help but think of a place we used to go as kids, it was one of Akuma's favorite places to go. It's near the beach by the caves. I used to see there a lot when we were kids." Micheal said.

"What place would that be? There are not many places there other than the old Murphy house, it's been empty since we were little, but I remember it was one of Gregory's favorites because of the mining shafts but Micheal's favorite for other reasons." Skylar said looking at Micheal smiling.

"I thought you hated it there Micheal. Especially after it started to fall apart. Why would we go there?" I certainly enjoyed exploring the place but wouldn't call it my favorite.

"I used to bring girls back there, I always had one of the rooms made up so it would look romantic, it was one of the places Skylar and I fooled around in. But also, the Murphy's were friends of mom and dad, they were an older couple and knew our grandparents, their graves are out back but Akuma was interested in the place also, I thought there might be something there that could help us. I'm looking for anything possible." Micheal said.

"You two fooled around?" I asked.

"By now it's obvious, you were not going to do anything, and I certainly wasn't going to turn her down, look at her, she's sexy and I used to masturbate to the thought of her. Yes, I'm gross but I'm forward and honest, I'm younger so learn from me." Micheal said as he was half laughing.

"First we will look here, that way we don't spend time going back and forth in case we miss something, if no one is there then we can check the other place, either way I want to find her." I said.

"Before we leave, I'm grabbing my backpack, I have a few more things to add to it." Micheal said as he went to get it ready.

He refused to go anywhere without his backpack, it was something Mr. Murphy taught him, and he's always taken it with him ever since, it's a good thing because it's been needed.

# Chapter Fifteen

We made our way through the trees, the only road that made it to the island in the middle was empty, no cars or people standing outside. We made our way down the rope that was still in place, nothing had changed outside since we were here, Skylar kept looking for cameras which was a strange thing not to have with all the equipment and by now someone should have noticed our ropes, they were hidden slightly but were visible down below.

Opening the door, there wasn't anything in our path, going in we expected to see the clones to the side with the pool they generated from, except the pool itself was empty, all the equipment was gone, there wasn't tape so it wasn't marked off by the police, there were no indicators anyone was ever here other than the building and elevator. The other room they had left in before was left open, being careful not to walk into a trap, looking in, the room was empty, but we did notice there was another door. Opening it, there was only a stairwell leading up.

"She certainly cleared this place out even though it would have been the safest place, I doubt there is enough space at the Murphy place, I wonder where she could have taken it all. I doubt she would want to go far if she's desperate to get Gregory." Skylar said.

"I don't know much about her other than when she was around when Skylar scribed the ancient book on me. She said that back in the cave on the first night when all of that started happening. I'm surprised she didn't take me then, she had plenty of opportunities to take control over me, heck, she had me tied up and could do anything she wanted. Why didn't she?" I don't know why I hadn't thought about that until now.

"Maybe she was hoping if she put you through one of your fantasies or showed you what you could get, maybe you would help her willingly or be a partner with her?" Micheal said.

"Most of the time we spoke, she insulted me, she was less

impressed with me than a person would be of an ostrich.

"Is there anything else you are holding back, you made it seem like all they did was ask a couple lame questions, tying you up and having sex maybe once." Skylar frowned at me.

"I was embarrassed, its why I asked if others thought I was gay and both you and Micheal said you helped the rumors. Yes I had sex with Akuma, I assume I did, not that I saw her, actually I believe Eisheth's clone did which is now Nova, after that there was a second night and that night was a bunch of male clones, you can guess from that, then when this party started, Micheal wasn't in one of the rooms but you saw me through the two way mirror with another guy, those are all the sex things that happened, and yes, I'll admit in front of my brother, I had sex with you when you were tied up waiting for your date. I admit when this started I hoped for an adventure, I thought she was just being creative, bringing out my inner fantasies and actually creating them, I felt drawn to her and if it had been just that, I admit I would keep doing it or see where it led, but unfortunately she's done all these other things and the fact she's killed people, that kills the mood." I felt frustrated but finally spilled it all out there.

"Before he tells us anymore. Let's take the vehicle, it will be much quicker." Micheal said as he left us standing there.

Over the next few hours, we collected the vehicle and drove towards our old town, we hadn't seen anyone, not even one vehicle leaving or coming to town. Instead of going into town, we deviated down one of the two track dirt roads heading towards the Murphy house. It was directly on the lake, there were three homes there and all had been emptied for years, one of them had an old mining shaft which would be a better lead since Akuma would need a place to hide things. Unfortunately, living in a mountain town with several lakes and countless ponds, there were plenty of places to hide.

We had to park a short distance from the house, the road only went to a certain point and stopped. Getting out we looked around and watched the ground for footprints, so far nothing. Walking along the beach, we passed the area where they had the ceremony. The night we watched them from on top of the cliff, nothing was there, and the cave was empty also. We kept walking along the ridge of the back, then came to the private bridge that crossed the water to the other side. Following that, once we were on the other side, there were countless footprints along with long drawn lines along the ground. There was definitely new activity here.

None of the three houses were on the same level as the path that led upward, the third house was half built into the side of the rock and much higher than the lake level. The first home we came to was the old Ollerson home, when he was alive, he made wood furniture and inside there were still several pieces of furniture that he hand crafted, his clothes rotting away and a teacup with dried up herbs in it as if it was still waiting for him to return. The second house was the McMillton house, it was a little larger in size, if you were social and loved tea parties, they had them, either tea or book clubs, they invited guests over to play music and enjoy each other's company.

The second house had more footprints around it, but the Murphy house had the most. Their house was at the ridge where you couldn't go along the lake, but it was high enough to dive into the water. This side was part of the mountain while the other side was large rolling hills. We were trying to decide how to get into the house, there were several clones outside standing around by the old driveway to the north of the house. There were several clones standing around in the main house. As we came up to one of the windows closer to the rock wall, there was an empty room, but it was too close to the others. There used to be bars on the window and locks on the doors, so it was a safe guess Akuma took this place over. We wanted to get up to the roof, enter the small door there into the attic and if we could, take the dumbwaiter down. It could hold five hundred pounds and pass the second and first floors going down to the basement.

Small parts of where the house was built into the rock, there were uneven and small enough areas to place your hands to get a grip, pulling up and keeping one foot on the house and one foot on the rock, it helped with climbing up. I was the first to go up with Skylar second and Micheal followed. Getting to the top and pulling myself over, I helped both Skylar and Micheal. There was a small door that led to stairs that would normally go all the way down and lead through the kitchen to the first floor. Instead, we went in onto the third floor of the house, took the dumbwaiter, barely squeeing in since it was meant for groceries, tools or other household items and not people. We slowly slid down, second and first floors were quiet, no one was talking but if it was only the clones they wouldn't talk.

We lowered ourselves down to the basement, where there wasn't any light. Slowly lifting the door, one at a time, we climbed out. There wasn't anything down here. We made our way to the far back part of the house where they had a closet, opening the door slowly and looking in, there wasn't anyone waiting either. There was still old clothing hanging to hide the second door. The back door in the closet led to the old mining shaft. It wasn't registered and very few people knew and after it was closed and the owners passed away, no one really cared since it was left abandoned with the rest of the house closing it off from the outside, at least there used to be locks and bars on the windows.

Once we opened the door, the track for the mining carts that led straight down wasn't there, we last saw it three years ago so they might be using it to lower things. We slowly walked down on the track, there were four levels before it became too steep, then we moved over to one of the drifts, they had various drifts that would go back and forth leading to lower levels of the mining area. Thankfully none of them had caved in.

There were bright glowing lights that we didn't need our flashlights. They hadn't used the natural lighting no doubt to prevent some of the clones from bursting. There were torches leading down, thankfully there wasn't any natural gas leaking down here or there would be a serious problem. There were new beams reinforcing the walls along with cement to harden the floors and sides. You could see old gobbing stacked up along the sides, the way old miners would use rocks and other pieces to recreate walls or to reinforce the ceiling, it also helped get extra pieces out of the way. When we came to the end of the shaft before it turned the corner and went down further, I was curious about the old workstation. Behind the door on the wall, there was a medium size room with a bench and several tools to fix winches, pulleys, trollies or anything else they needed. They also stored oil and other items; dynamite was stored much lower.

Instead of seeing any of that rusting away or covered in dust, there was a smooth floor with several people sitting on the floor with blindfolds on and their feet and hands bound. We recognized one of them as one of our local sheriffs, not that we had a plan, but we knew we needed to let them go, if anything they might help or know more current information about what Akuma was doing or if she was here. Untying the sheriff, we started on the others. Keeping everyone in the room for now we asked.

"Did Akuma bring you here or something else?" I asked.

"It was your brother Micheal." Everyone pointed at him angrily.

"I promise it wasn't me, there are clones made of us, but we thought we took all of them. Akuma must have made more." Micheal said.

"I don't fall for games, you will be serving an extremely long time in jail for those you either harmed or killed, so far its looking like life without parole." The Sheriff stated.

"I promise my brother has been with us the entire time and we can prove its not him." Making sure no one was near us, we helped get everyone out.

Standing on the side of the house, Micheal lured one of the clones over that looked like me, everyone was shocked and wondering if I had a secret twin. When they saw Micheal could only give him certain directions and didn't speak, they thought we were still trying to fool them. I was able to ask the clone to explain himself even though we knew the others still didn't believe it. It wasn't until Skylar pulled his arm from his socket and separated it from his body, causing the others to look on in shock.

"If he had been real, there would be blood everywhere or at least he would be screaming in pain. These clones do not show expression or feel pain. There's a lot more but we need to get to the bottom of the mining shafts. I promise when we figure out where Akuma is, we can explain the rest of this, but Micheal isn't responsible." I stated.

The sheriff assisted the others safely to the bridge and back into town while we made our way back down the various rifts until we came to the last shaft. There were two metal doors, something that wasn't down here before. Both were locked and we couldn't pick them. Instead, we climbed up on one of the strong thick beams they used to reinforce the tunnel waiting for someone to come out. It took a couple hours of waiting until there was a person who came out, while they walked away from the door, Micheal lowered a bath towel to keep the door from fully latching completely.

"I knew I would use it eventually, if that wasn't a clone they would have seen us." He whispered to us.

After the person left, we dropped down and opened the door, there was another hallway and several doors that led off in several directions. Akuma seemed to like labyrinth styles and incorporated them into each of her bases. A few of the doors had a tiny window and we could see most of the rooms housed more clones and we found more that were ours, she must have something left over from us even though she never took blood from us, at least that we were aware of.

All her equipment had been moved here laid out along each wall with one pocket carved out with several clones standing motionless. None of her followers were with her which made us wonder if she killed them all off. Then we had a chance to see how many clones she has been busy making. The far wall had been fake, lifting, it revealed a large room with possibly two thousand clones. She was flashing various lights at them, only a few burst while others either started twitching or slightly deformed. Rounding them up, she placed them back in the large vat which they went back to their original liquid form. She was reusing them this time trying to get the results she wanted. She gave orders to one of the clones to go up and collect a person from the holding cell, which was good we already released them, who knows how many she already killed trying to get what she wanted but where was she putting the bodies, we doubted she was letting them loose anymore.

Akuma kept looking over her notes, looking frustrated as she dowsed her clones with something and testing the electric shock on them, not getting what she wanted, they were repeatedly dissolved. Many of the clones she was running through were of people we had never seen before wondering where the original was, unless there were some, she let go like Micheal which we assume she regrets now.

# Chapter Sixteen

"I know neither of you will like this, but you'll need to trust me. I have my cell phone, and I'll do my best to keep you updated, if she takes it, I still have the tracker on me but trust me." I whispered to them.

I hoped they would trust me and let me do this even if it looked like I lost my sanity. Moving further out of sight since we knew she would be looking to see if anyone came with me. I dropped down slowly and walked up into the room with Akuma, she was so engrossed with what she was doing or assumed the only one who would be walking in would be one of her clones.

"I see your still working on the clone creations." I said to get her attention.

She looked at me shocked to see me standing there, not something she thought would happen without forcing me.

"Is that you or one of my clones?" She asked.

"Definitely an original. I've been studying the clones, there are so many possibilities to them, many are difficult to tell if they are real or not. When you started the game in the cave, I thought it was simply someone wanting to live out their fantasies and I wanted something to distract me, which you managed to do. I thought it was you I was with, but I found out it wasn't you. I had no idea they were so lifelike. What I don't understand is why you want me, you used to insult and put me down as if dust had more value, so why would you want me? How could I possibly help make this any better?" I hoped to get her to slowly trust me.

"Are you truly alone?" Akuma asked as she looked around.

"I am alone, if they had known I wanted to come here to speak with you, I wouldn't be here. I couldn't help it, I find myself obsessed with the clones, why did you make it so they would only talk to me, you didn't make it so you could track them to me if they saw me, so why give me control over them?" I didn't want to ask too many questions.

110

"My plans haven't exactly gone according to plan. I've had so much slow me down, especially recently. But now that you're here, maybe you might be willing to work with me." Akuma still sounded skeptical.

I walked over to one of the clones lifting their hand, inspecting their hands, fingers and nails. I still couldn't get over how realistic they were, if they had expression, it would be even more difficult to tell the difference.

"Depending on how skilled they are, they could be taught to do dangerous jobs saving lives or volunteering when help is needed but not enough people around that can do it. One of the clones I was observing was able to rename herself when asked, it was based on something I liked and information about me but the fact she chose the name for herself, shows progress." I said.

"I knew out of everyone you would understand my vision better than anyone else. These simple minds keep preventing me from doing such good, getting excuses to why I can't create clones saying its tampering with natural life, that who am I to decide when something lives. Its no different than getting pregnant and having a child, but this way we start with full grown adults and they can be useful immediately, any learning is programmed directly into them, fiber optics helps make it possible to get signals all throughout the body, but with your DNA I can make the organs grow so people can use their body parts and these creations cannot feel any pain. None of that bothers you, does it?" Akuma watched for any expressions that I might give.

"I honestly can't see anything wrong with any of that. What I don't understand is why are some of them ending up wonky, I don't know if you are aware of it, but the news keeps finding these people and they say they are testing as human but are incapable of speaking or communicating in any way, but they don't appear to be the clones?" I wondered if she would own up to killing people.

"I've had a few glitches and inconveniences. I need to show you something." Was all she said.

She went over and picked up a syringe, tied a band around her arm and took a small amount of blood, then she grabbed another syringe and tied a tight band around my arm and took a tiny piece of blood from me. Then she started up the machine, pushing a few buttons at the console, the water in the corner started to bubble, she directly dropped the blood from the syringes into the water causing an interesting person from the water to take shape and now stepping out of the water.

"Did you choose his look, or did it become this from our DNA?" I would be impressed if she was able to create brand new people.

"If we had a child together, this is what he would look like." She directed him over to the foam pad.

Flipping the switch that sent the bolt of electricity through him, he simply twitched a little but did not burst like many had or slump and fall over. Once it was done, he looked at either of us and stepped off from the pad, he looked like he had shown more expression than any of the others. I was impressed, if it hadn't been for killing others, this wouldn't have been a problem.

"I admit I am rather impressed. I know people who would love to have a clone of their own. Anything can be used in a horrible way, but this truly is a better alternative to others that have been suggested." I had no idea why she would need to kill anyone over this, I couldn't see the draw back.

"During the experimental period I had to do some questionable things to make this work. Your parents refused to share their invention, so I had to sort of learn how to create this on my own. This could bring me so much power and money." She sounded rather excited.

"I wish you would have approached me earlier about this, I would have tried helping with funding, I'm sure it wasn't cheap. Don't get me wrong, I enjoyed the adventure in the cave, normally it was something I would never do, but I found I really enjoyed it. But this would be worth funding." I wished she could have approached this whole thing differently.

"I didn't want to risk anyone stopping me simply because they didn't like the concept of others being used who can't give permission, people refused to give me things simply because it wasn't benefiting them. I stole what I needed, one of these medical devices cost me one million dollars, I had to kill the person who tried to stop me from leaving with it, but it was for the better good. I won't let people step all over me anymore, they will no longer look down on me and tell me what I can and cannot do, I can make the rules now to life. No one controls me anymore." The expression on her face was a little scary.

"You killed a person to get medical equipment? I'm sure we could have found a way to rent or make payments for one, companies will sell theirs used." I was surprised something minor like that she would have killed someone over.

"He's not the only one, I killed four people who used to bully me, but no one will ever know they are not there anymore, there are clones in their places. Plus a few people who refused to let me use their likeness for clones, apparently, they didn't like the idea of strangers having sex with something that looked identical to them. A bit ironic, my sister was against it, but her clone worked out so much better, but I lost that one somewhere." She sounded disappointed.

"Have you sold any clones so far?" I was curious how many she might have if she was willing to share the information on them.

"I've successfully sold eight hundred captivating sex dolls, each a unique creation of art and desire; however, they are regrettably limited in their capabilities. If only I could unlock the potential for them to communicate with their owners—imagine how much more valuable they would become! Presently, their functionality is confined to the tasks programmed into their control boxes, leaving them as mere shadows of what they could be. With access to additional information and advanced technology, I could rewire these controls and elevate these lifelike figures into something truly extraordinary. However, there are obstacles that hinder my progress." She said sounding frustrated.

"Have they never talked?" I was surprised they didn't speak to her.

"As a child, I was acutely aware of their remarkable ability to communicate; I had witnessed them engaging in open and animated conversations with our parents, exchanging thoughts and ideas as if they were equals. In those moments, my parents seemed utterly oblivious to the extraordinary nature of what unfolded before their eyes, focused solely on their own desires and interpretations—trapped in a narrow view that relegated these intelligent beings to mere objects for gratification. The profound connection we shared was lost on them amidst their preoccupation with superficial pleasures. While your parents crafted a digital companion designed to be your ultimate best friend—one who spoke on your behalf and tailored responses just for you—the entity you referred to, as her only recently adopted the name Nora. This is not merely a whim or personal decision; rather, it's an intricate selection process dictated by an algorithm that refined its interactions based upon data collected about you, ultimately narrowing down the vast possibilities to this singular choice. It all comes down to complex programming tied to one simple name—a designation I am powerless to alter, no matter how deeply I wish for something more human at its core." Akuma clenched her fist.

"Unfortunately, I don't remember any of this stuff existing. My parents raised us to be perfectly average kids, nothing out of the ordinary ever happened and if it did then I must have been oblivious to it." So far, I was being honest with her since she kept watching for every muscle movement I made with my expressions.

"My parents had a lab but unfortunately, I forgot where they kept it. I looked in their summer home, a few in other places but could not find it. They loved the old Murphy home but other then the mine shafts and the materials they used to pull out of here, there was nothing special, but you and your brother Micheal loved being here. The cave was another special place. I hoped by sparking your inner desires, it might bring something back. I might as well tell you the secret I said I knew about you." Akuma went and sat down by the console.

"I am curious since you brought it up but never answered." I assumed it was when I was changed but she knew I was aware of that, we already talked about it.

"Back when we were just eleven years old, everything seemed so simple—until that fateful accident turned our world upside down. Your parents, in their worry, barred me from playing with you any longer, claiming that I wasn't a good friend. But how could they understand what truly happened? It wasn't my fault that your head collided with the pavement; an unfortunate twist of fate left you with a concussion and fragments of memories scattered like leaves on the wind. Perhaps it is this foggy recollection that dims your understanding now. And while my occasional teasing may come off as an insult, if only you knew— it was merely my clumsy attempt to express the deep fascination or rather obsession I had for you even then. As children often do, I found myself captivated by your laughter and spirit; it was an obsession rooted in innocence and longing for connection—a feeling entirely outside my control at such a tender age. If I wanted to kill or harm you, I've had plenty of chances to do it." Akuma sat there smiling at me.

"I appreciate that you didn't kill or harm me. If' I'm understanding correctly, when you say obsession, you mean you had a crush on me?" I wasn't sure what else to say to her.

"What I felt for you transcended mere infatuation; it was a deep, abiding desire to be with you that went beyond childish yearnings—I longed to call you mine in every sense. Yet, time and again, my hopes were dashed as I watched you fawn over that blonde girl who seemed to capture your every glance and thought. In those moments of palpable frustration, a wild idea took root in my mind: if only I could create a doppelgänger of you—one who would match your dazzling charm but be entirely devoted to me. She could keep the simulacrum while I cherished the authentic connection we shared. To me, you were nothing short of my soulmate—a sentiment so profound that even those around me shook their heads in disbelief at what they deemed insanity. And perhaps they weren't wrong; after all, wasn't your relentless fixation on her just as deranged? You trailed her like a shadow, granting her unearned grace and indulgence at every turn while ignoring my longing heart. But despite their skepticism and laughter behind closed doors, I eventually proved them wrong—I turned their mockery into an unexpected lesson about love's complexities and its overpowering grip on our lives. I taught them all a lesson. If I wanted something, I had to be determined. Perhaps we could uncover where my parents hid their lab —it's crucial for my project. But first, I've got some bodies to attend to." Akuma said with no reflection in her voice.

"Do you need help, maybe I could help you with the bodies, if they are heavy, I am strong." Not that I wanted to see dead people, but I could find out where they were being buried.

"You are just far too adorable to be getting your hands dirty in such a messy situation! Why don't you stay right here and manage the clones while I take care of the, shall we say, less pleasant tasks involving the bodies? Don't worry; I promise to return before you know it. And I can just imagine how much you're going to miss me during my brief absence! But until then, perhaps one of those delightful clones would be more than happy to offer you some pleasure while you're waiting for my triumphant return. Consider it a thrilling distraction" Akuma was about to leave me there.

"You haven't shown me how to operate the console unless it works on its own." I hoped to distract her long enough when I hoped Micheal and Skylar would get the same idea I was.

"It's a straightforward process involving these rather mischievous puppets. If they seem out of sorts or decide that lounging by the water pit is far more entertaining than behaving like obedient little clones, simply give them a gentle prod and send them back for another dip in the watery depths! Luckily for you, the console takes care of all the heavy lifting—think of it as your personal assistant with no coffee breaks required. Should that pesky button flash red like an excited cherry tomato, just give it a quick push; voila! The whole operation will spring back to life again... but only if one of those feisty clones gets themselves hilariously stuck." She walked over to me, giving me a rather firm kiss on the lips, she left me standing there, watching her leave.

# Chapter Seventeen

Pulling out my cell phone I saw the text my brother sent me, it let me know they put the tracker on her vehicle so we could find out where she was going to bury the bodies. That it was safe for me to come out. Placing my phone in my pocket, I tried to get out.

Pulling at the door, it refused to budge, somehow it locked even though we never saw one on the other side and I couldn't find one on this side. I sent a message letting Micheal know I was stuck in here. He let me know they had the recording of Akuma while we were talking, that her admitting to murders and more, they and the police were going to follow her and once they caught up to her, catching her in the act of burying one of the bodies or one in her possession, they were going to arrest her and would be back for me. Not that I liked the idea of being stuck in here. At least it was safe, and the clones wouldn't do anything to me, it still creeped me out a little.

I sat in the seat watching each clone automatically march down a hallway, only a few fell backwards, at least I didn't have to touch them, they were missing a leg causing them to fall back into the fluid. Getting up, I figured they were good enough on their own, I wanted to see where this tunnel went since it was newly built from the last time I was down here. What I did question was the clone who followed me, the one Akuma whispered something to that kept following me around. I was concerned what she might have said to it.

There was no door the clones had to deal with, going down a declined walkway until it opened into another room, the largest yet and each cloned single file stood in a row automatically stacking themselves waiting for orders. There was plenty of space to walk around so she expected to use this to house the majority of her clones, there were so many faces of people I had never seen before. Taking the small flashlight from my belt, I flashed it around the room to see how many would burst and which ones were solid enough to stay. Not one of them burst.

Counting each one, there were twelve hundred. Only two hundred were duplicates of Skylar, Micheal and me.

The clone following me stood behind me which made me nervous, I turned, and it kept trying to get behind me. I walked around looking more at the other clones, I guessed at least another two thousand could fit down here before it filled up. Going back up to the main area, there were filing cabinets, some were locked while others were not. I checked the files that were on the top first, and it looked like a few of them had large orders. I also found the papers with the mixture for the water, and it listed at the bottom several question marks where the missing components were and what she thought it was. Thankfully she didn't know we already knew where my parent's laboratory was.

I not only found a disk to upgrade their software but also several other important files that explained from beginning to end the process of what our parents had been working on. In the diary I read it explained what an amazing opportunity it was, but they would discontinue the project after finding out how dangerous it could be stating instability. Unfortunately, there wasn't more listed since it was the last journal entry made.

I kept checking my phone, but no one had sent me any new messages. I began to wonder how they were and hopefully hadn't fallen for any traps of hers. The clone with me finally got behind me and started to massage my shoulders. It felt good but I wasn't in the mood for it to go any further, especially right now.

He reached around trying to grab my penis, instead I grabbed his hand and turned around to face him.

"The Gregory you are supposed to pleasure is over there by the printing machine." I said not sure if he would continue to bother me or not.

"I am ordered to pleasure Gregory." He said as he left me and went to the other clone. It felt strange watching a clone of myself pleasuring another clone of myself.

Looking around, there hadn't been any windows, old doors that might have led to other mining shafts, the original owners I don't think ever went down this far. I was feeling claustrophobic in here. I watched as the others continued to line up. After all of this was over, I had no idea what was going to be done with the clones, not that we needed more. Looking at the console, I noticed a small button. Curious, I went ahead and pushed it. The cloning process stopped and no more were coming out of the orange water. I looked around to see what clone might be the most intelligent or at least someone I might get a few answers from.

I noticed that my two clones were getting extremely comfortable with each other, a true live sex show right here just for me. Going over to one of the female clones I had never seen before I asked her.

"You might not know, but is there a way out of here?" I was desperate for anything.

I was already down here for six hours. There was nothing left to read or search through, I had gone through the desk, filing cabinets and everything else. I was even bored enough to touch the orange water; it formed a finger on my hand that fell back in and dissolved. I wished I knew what was taking them so long. My cell phone service kept coming and going but my text finally went through asking them how it was going. The text I received back didn't sound too good. She realized they were following her and ditched them, but they did drive by a site that had freshly dug dirt, it was one of the areas she had been burying bodies in. Now they were trying to locate her and said if they couldn't find her, they would be back in an hour to get me.

I started to hear noise so I texted back that she was already back here, she must have driven around the long way so she wouldn't have to go back past them. Then I hid my phone so she wouldn't know I had it on me.

The door opened and Akuma came in, but she wasn't wearing the same outfit she left in, this time she looked like she was wearing a bride's dress but all black with red blood stains on it. She brushed her dress off and went over to the machine, it didn't seem to bother her that the machine stopped and wasn't producing anymore people. She pulled a vial from her purse and went over dropping it into the water and then turned the console back on. Watching it, there was a very distinguished gentleman who came out of the water. Once he had, she dressed him in a suit and tie, giving him a piece of paper to read.

"My dress was stunning before this unfortunate incident; however, it now bears an unwelcome mark of blood because the preacher refused to return willingly and perform our wedding ceremony as promised. Despite the unforeseen circumstances, I want you to know that what you're wearing is perfectly fine—it doesn't diminish my excitement in the least. I can hardly contain my anticipation at the thought of soon hearing you call me your wife. My heart races at the prospect of joining our lives together, no matter how chaotic things have become today." She smiled at me, all excited as she pulled a podium out for him to stand behind.

"We are getting married?" I wasn't expecting this.

"Naturally, my dear, we are getting married—you must know

that this isn't some fleeting whim, or a joke played on you. We've been weaving our dreams of togetherness since childhood when we first envisioned our lives intertwined like the vines of an unyielding jungle. It's not as if I've fabricated this grand plan out of thin air; no, we've meticulously laid each brick in the foundation of our shared destiny with the fervor only true love can inspire. I promise you a life filled with exhilaration and joy beyond your wildest fantasies—a joyful existence unmarred by outside forces or disapproving glances from friends and family who don't understand what we share. Nothing will stand between us; nothing at all will derail the inexorable march towards our blissful future! Now tell the preacher to start reading." Akuma linked her arm with mine pulling me in front of him.

I doubted this was even legal since we didn't have any papers, but I certainly wouldn't willingly marry her. But I also didn't want to end up like the preacher which I'm pretty sure she is admitting to killing. I had to fill time until the others got here and hopefully, they were not going to wait a full hour, I wasn't sure how I was going to survive this.

"Preacher, please read the paper." At least for now I intended on playing along to keep her happy.

"We are here to witness the marriage of Akuma Elizabeth Corwell to Gregory Thomas Atwood. They have their vows written and we will now hear them." The clone stopped and waited for us to speak.

Akuma handed me a folded piece of paper, as she did, she unfolded her own and was now reading her own vows. I was curious what she wrote for me.

"From the very first moment our eyes locked and the world around us faded into oblivion, I felt an unshakeable certainty deep within my soul—that you were destined to be my forever. It was as if every fiber of my being whispered your name, compelling me with an insatiable desire to claim you for myself, no matter what extremes I might have to endure. Driven by this relentless passion that coursed through my veins like a potent drug, I resolved in that instant to weave our fates together. From this day forward and for all eternity, know that my heart belongs solely and irrevocably to you—a captive in the beautiful madness of love that has ensnared us both. Now you read yours." She smiled as she couldn't wait to hear the words come from my own lips.

. Taking a deep breath, I looked at the paper, she had written something I never would have said to her. Continuing to play along for now, I read her paper she gave me.

"If I were granted the chance to have you by my side for all eternity, I would deem every single moment a life exquisitely worthy of living; your presence is the very essence that ignites my soul. Not a fragment of me desires to navigate through this chaotic world without you—my heart rebels against such an abominable thought. The reality we create together forms the foundation of my perfect existence, spun from dreams and tinged with madness. Akuma, in a world full of fleeting choices and transient affections, it is unequivocally you that I choose above all else. My devotion knows no bounds; it spirals into obsession as every heartbeat whispers your name like a dark lullaby in the night—a haunting melody that draws me ever closer to you." I was at a loss for words after reading it.

"Tell the preacher to continue." Akuma said.

"Preacher, please continue." I asked.

"From the power invested in me from the internet and the great state of earth, I pronounce you husband and wife. You may now kiss the bride." The preacher clone stated.

I turned to see Akuma lift her veil off from her face, she was beautiful, there was no mistaking that. Tall, flowing long blonde hair, heart shaped lips and a body that I knew I enjoyed, but having her pretend to marry me, this all felt very strange, especially since killing a person didn't seem to bother her at all. Not wanting to upset her, I placed my hand around her waist and pulled her towards me, placed my other hand under her chin, tipped it and kissed her on the lips. I wasn't sure what she had planned after this, but I kept wishing any moment the police or Micheal and Skylar would burst in and stop this madness.

"So, where should we take our honeymoon?" At least if she planned on somewhere else, we could get out of this place and maybe I could escape.

"I'm about to whisk you away to your most cherished sanctuary in this vast universe: an enchanting bedroom jungle honeymoon, where every corner bursts with wild exoticism and passion that mirrors the intoxicating chaos of our hearts." She said excitedly.

I was afraid she would say something like that. She took me by the hand and walked me over to one of the tall filing cabinets, pulling it out, there was a room revealed behind it. There were vines creeping down the sides of the walls, bushes and mini fake trees, there was a platform that went out to the center of the room to a heart shaped bed. Surrounded by a ring of orange water. It seemed to be everywhere now. I swear if I never saw this type of water again, I would be incredibly happy. She was about to close the cabinet closing off the other room when I stopped her.

"Leave it open, the clones can watch." I hoped it would turn her on or at least be enticing.

The last thing I wanted was to be stuck in here and not have the others know there was a room back here, I spent six hours searching the place, and I had no idea it was back here. She held onto my hand as she led me in.

"I'm amazed you had enough time to make it look this amazing." Other than the creepy water, it was an interesting room.

"Nothing but the finest for you my sweet. While you were chasing that hussy, I've been preparing our future together. All of this was done for you." Akuma said while smiling.

"The clones, the rooms down here and other places, all of that was for me?" I doubted all of this could have been for me.

"The clones helped me dig out and build these places, they also decorated them. You have no idea how many I lost from mining cave ins or simply being destroyed one way or another. I went through thousands of clones, especially when they were not as equipped the way they are now, the money from selling many of them made all this possible, the money gives us power and control. Once I kill Skylar, then there won't be absolutely anything in our way. It will feel so good to have her last breath escape between my fingers." Akuma was satisfied with herself.

That's when I started to feel dizzy, all this time when I kept seeing Skylar on the ground dying, it was because of Akuma, if she had the chance to get closer to me, it's when Skylar died. Similar to a daydream, I started to see Skylar in the mining shaft dying but it always seemed to stop when Akuma had me. This wasn't like me and not the type of thing I would do, but I had to try. I did something I wasn't expecting, I closed the door, if Akuma couldn't get out, then she couldn't lay her hands on Skylar.

"I'm confused, I thought you wanted that open?" Akuma looked surprised.

"I changed my mind; I want you all to myself." Everything she's done has creeped me out, but I kept trying to get that feeling back when I had no idea what was behind all of this, and it was simply getting tied up by a stranger.

If I could trust a stranger I was going to have to wait and find out what I was going to do with her. Maybe if she had me willingly then maybe the appeal would be ruined for her. If she wanted a husband, then she was going to have one.

# Chapter Eighteen

I was fully aware of the daunting task ahead; it was like staring down a dragon while holding nothing but a dandelion and a wild imagination. This mission wasn't going to be any walk in the park—it would teeter more towards an uphill hike through brambles, complete with pesky mosquitoes and that one friend who constantly gets side-tracked by squirrels. It wasn't just about persuading myself; I had to pull out all the persuasive stops to convince Akuma too! Little did I know just how attached she was to this enigmatic place—or if she'd simply taken root there, thinking she'd planted flowers instead of forging off into what felt like an epic quest where half my brain began chanting "Not again!" So, there I sat on this imaginary couch, mentally grappling with whether we were truly brave adventurers or just unsuspecting victims lured into chaos—but as much as it took convincing both my skeptical reflection and her brightly determined eyes, deep down I realized that sometimes you simply must embrace discomfort for whatever nightmare filled mischief awaited us at our destination! I had to think like Akuma.

"I'm surprised you didn't take us to the ultimate location, I appreciate how romantic this place is but the one place we all knew and loved as children. There's a cabin at the top of the mountain, where after being bullied we would go there for peace, it was like a second home. To be there with you would have been perfect." I said wistfully.

"We can still do that; this place will be our main home, but we can go anywhere that makes you happy." Akuma said as she scooped the end of her dress and opening the door.

"You truly don't mind giving up this vision of perfection for a true unification of us?" I asked.

"I don't mind but there are a few things that will need to come with us." Smiling at me she went out to the main room.

She ordered several clones to carry the pool of water, once she drained the water and folded it up, then a few carried a large barrel of the liquid and followed us as we made out way out of the mine. I would have preferred to go up to the cabin without all the medical equipment and especially without the clones but at least we were moving away from where Skylar could be hurt or my brother. There were so many abandoned cabins all throughout the mountains, some to get away and others where they had hidden mining shafts. When we made our way out of the mining shaft to the outdoors, we still hadn't seen anyone, it shouldn't have taken the others this long to get here.

We followed along a path that might have been used years ago but was overgrown now, especially with a few trees falling over. Watching the way Akuma ordered the clones ahead of us to clear the pathway was like watching henchmen wipe everything out making a clear path. If anyone had seen what was around us, they would know something had been through here recently because of us. Interesting how something so small as speaking irritated her, yet she could get them to follow her orders. We passed several cabins that had roofs collapse from years of neglect. I was surprised Akuma hadn't asked once to find out if any of those were the one I spoke of. There was one Michael, and I used to hide in, and play pretend in when we were younger, no one lived in it at that time either. After walking a while we could see it in the distance, and I was rather shocked to see how new it looked.

"I knew how much it meant to you, so I took care of it after all these years." Akuma announced proudly.

She had the door opened and inside it was perfectly decorated with items that Micheal and I had discarded throughout our lives; she must have been rummaging through our trash without any of us having any clue. On the rocking chair in the corner sat a teddy bear I had when I was six years old, my father bought it for me when I was sick. Next to the rocking chair that belonged to my mom, was the dog cage that held my stuff animal, my parents didn't feel I was responsible enough for a real one yet. It was one of those moments you felt both horrified and impressed at the same time. The only thing that was new had been the new room I added to my place last year, she replicated it here. The natural plant pool glass dome style accessible through the kitchen, she did the same here and the bedroom upstairs decorated the same and with the small balcony to overlook the new room below.

I can't believe you did all of this for me. If anyone had done something like this for me, I would have given them the chance of a relationship with me.

I would have felt honored but the part of her killing people with no remorse and planning on killing more simply to remove what she thought was competition, that ruined it. I watched as she had the clones place her creepy pool in the corner of the living room. Akuma noticed that I was watching it when she told me.

"I like having it around for my beauty treatments, it keeps me young looking. I'll have them fix up the basement, so I won't have to haul this up, I have several in other locations." As she said it, one of the clones had a mishap.

The clone was setting down one of her heavy boxes trapping his arm underneath, instead of waiting for it to be pulled back so he could get his arm off, his arm detached. Akuma didn't hide her frustration and tossed the clone and his arm into the water dissolving them. When she looked at her arm she frowned for a second when she dipped her finger in the water and ran it over her arm. Rubbing her arm slightly she seemed happy again. Smiling at me, she took my hand leading me into the bedroom and closed the door behind.

"Do you enjoy this more when your being blindfolded, or do you want to try something different?" Akuma asked.

"As long as no other men are participating, I'm always up for trying something new. But for now, I'm more excited to see you out of that gown." I said.

"Will you help me undress, it has so many buttons down the back that I can't reach." Akuma turned around showing me the back of the dress.

It was a beautiful dress; I had never seen a bridal gown in black before. Chapel length, elegant and timeless A-line silhouette with satin gown with intricate lace overlaying. Sweetheart neckline with no sleeves, tiny pearl beads down the back. Once it was unhooked, she let it drop to the floor. There was a hair in front of her face, as I slid it back behind her ear, I felt how soft her skin was. Placing my hand on her cheek, I leaned in and gave her a gentle kiss on the lips. She didn't react as most would when kissing, it was the part of what I enjoyed the most, it let me know where to go from here. Whether it was a quick romp in bed or a slow love session.

"If you're not feeling well, we can take our time, we don't have to rush into it. I know you've been busy getting a lot done." I was curious how she would react.

"Absolutely not! When it comes to marital bliss, consummation reigns supreme as the most essential ingredient in a successful union— because let's be honest, no amount of cake can compare to that magical moment when two lovebirds transform into a fully-fledged couple ready to take on the world together! After this, we have the fun and chaotic task of creating little bundles of joy—children who, unlike their adult counterparts, are far less likely to turn down a wild idea or an adventurous proposal." She stated while smiling.

"Most couples want to be married for a while before they have children. Do you plan on creating them naturally or cloning them?" I didn't like the direction this was taking.

"Naturally, they would be clones—why bother with the tedious and time-consuming process of training them when we could have ready-made perfection right out of the box? They'll come fully equipped with all the skills we desire, looking just as fabulous as we envisioned. And if, heaven forbid, they don't meet our unrealistic beauty standards or exhibit even the slightest imperfection, replacing them will be as straightforward and hassle-free as swapping out a mismatched sock! With a simple click of a button—or perhaps a sassy wave of the hand—we can conjure up an entirely new batch that fits our whims perfectly." Akuma sounded excited.

"Most prefer watching them learn new milestones and the imperfections is what makes us interesting as adults. We have so many years ahead of us, we don't need to worry about having children any time soon." I hoped to get her mind off of it.

"Not to worry, I already have samples. I can show you a preview." Akuma sounded excited as she started to look through her briefcase of glass vials.

"Don't those need to be temperature controlled?" I was surprised to see so many blood vials in a large case.

"It is temperature controlled, I made this myself to preserve anything put in it. I still have blood from you saved." Not waiting for my response, she was already dropping blood into the water.

The person didn't come out of the water as fast as the others did, it formed much slower, probably because it didn't have the full machine to progress it faster. What I was surprised by was that it wasn't a small child, it was a teenager.

"They start out as teens?" I was confused.

"Even if they happen to be flawless replicas in every conceivable way, their smaller stature renders them incapable of transporting heavy equipment effectively; the weight of necessity is simply too much for their diminutive frames to handle. The only problem I have is when you mix DNA from various people you tend to get more than one at a time." She was happy as three of them came out from the water.

"And you think this is the right way to start a family? So are the rest of the clone's family?" I was curious how she felt about the other clones of myself.

"Are you getting jealous? You will always be worth more than the clones; you have blood which clones don't have, and you have something they don't have. Ancient runes inscribed into you which make these clones much more valuable." She stated.

She grabbed clothes and draped them over the ones who came out. That's when I noticed a piece of her skin was slightly peeled.

"I would feel strange dropping them back in the goo, does it still work the same way if it's not connected to the console? Did you get hurt scratching yourself on the old door coming in?" I was concerned.

"Don't worry, it's nothing that a little water magic can't sort out! These two boys look so identical that I could swear they just stepped off the same assembly line. We'll happily keep one of them along with our lovely girl here because, let's face it, we need some variety in our lineup. But this particular twin? Well, he can take a scenic swim back to where he came from," she pushed the one in and he slowly dissolved, much slower without the electricity pulsing through the water, "all I have to do is sprinkle a few drops of water, and like magic, it transforms and repairs itself; it's astonishingly beneficial because this elixir has the incredible power to either mend or obliterate. However, this little-known secret is not something you're meant to uncover." Akuma seemed happy until she realized what she told me.

"It's a good thing you told me, husbands and wives don't keep secrets from each other, it has to feel good telling me, that way you don't have to question the way you talk anymore and worry if you're going to give something away." I hoped this explanation would calm her down.

"No, that certainly doesn't sound appealing. It seems we have reached an impasse with no alternative solutions at hand, despite the tremendous efforts I exerted to secure your presence here. Of course, there's always the option of keeping you confined in the basement—an unorthodox choice, perhaps, but one that could work quite well for me. In that shadowy sanctuary beneath my home, I could still draw your blood whenever necessary while ensuring your general well-being remains intact; after all, you'll be safe from the outside world in your secluded retreat... unless I happen to forget you're down there lost among those forgotten shadows, and maybe feeling a bit lonely missing out on life up here!" Akuma still sounded disappointed.

"It's not as if I'll tell anyone." I started to panic.

I picked this place because we used to store our toys here not that I saw any of the sharp objects, she must have cleared those out unless someone stole them assuming they were left behind by the previous owners. I couldn't lock her in the basement in the other place, she built it, she would know how to get out of it, and I didn't want to risk her being there after I had my vision again. I haven't had it since we came here so I knew it prevented it again for now. But the fact I figured out her huge secret, Akuma was a clone? Was that why my parents felt she was unsafe to be around, a clone who started to think for itself even if it was dangerous? Maybe she already replaced her family, we know what happened to her sister.

"I should kill you, but I need you and if I kill you then I only get so much blood. Clones, come here" She shouted.

"What are you doing?" I felt trapped and couldn't get out of the room.

"Clones, grab him and hold him still until we can chain him in the basement." She ordered them.

The clones came towards me trying to grab hold, when they had an order, they were certainly strong. I already learned that the hard way when Skylar told the one to penetrate me from behind. I hoped they might still respond to me when I spoke.

"Halt." I said quickly and to the point.

The clones stopped, with no expression it was difficult knowing if the order surprised them or they took my order over hers.

"Why are you stopping? Hold him down." She ordered again.

The clones started to move again towards me determined to carry out orders.

"Halt." I shouted again.

"They need to obey my orders; I've never had problems with them before." If Akuma had an expression to show, she would be stunned.

"They never had me here to give them orders. I'm not going to let them hold me down." I said.

"Well, it appears you've left me with no alternative; I'm afraid I must resort to the unthinkable and eliminate you." Akuma stated.

Akuma launched herself at me as I did my best to move out of the way. She was incredibly strong once she grabbed my arm. I kept twisting behind her so she couldn't get a better hold on me. We were getting closer to the water, and I didn't want to risk going in. It might not have done anything to me when I touched it and some of the clones it didn't dissolve.

"Clones, cover Akuma's mouth and help me put her in the water." I hoped it might do something with her, even if it only slowed her down.

The clones did exactly as I ordered, I barely had to touch her as they covered her mouth, she tried to speak but they couldn't hear her orders. Lifting her up off the ground, they set her down in the water. A few of the ones that helped had water splash on them dissolving them slightly. I hadn't expected anything to happen to Akuma as I tried to get into the other room. I planned on grabbing something I could tie her up with but there was no rope that I could see. What I noticed was her legs started to dissolve. That's when I asked.

"Remove your hand from her mouth. I thought the water wouldn't harm you since I saw you repair yourself with it?" I was confused.

"It's not electrified, it's the only thing that keeps me intact, pull me out, we can still work together, I can repair my legs. Clones, take me out of this." She asked.

"Clones, stop. Hold her in the water until she's partially dissolved." I know I wanted her to be finished but also, I needed something to show the police and have her pay for her crimes, I would let them deal with her.

Partly I kept thinking if she died, not that she was alive, there was so much I could still learn from her, that is if she was willing to fill me in. That and I hoped to find out who all the people she replaced with clones in their places. I knew I had my parents' notes but maybe if I understood what made her go the way she did, I could prevent others. There could still be a practical use for all these clones. She was now small enough I could handle her.

# Chapter Nineteen

Collecting all the clones that were at the cabin, I had them follow me as I had the pet carrier in my one hand. Walking through the woods was much easier than before since it was now cleared. In the distance I could see several officers and others inspecting the Murphy cabin. To the side my brother Micheal and Skylar looked on in concern and upset that they were not allowed to re-enter the cabin until their investigation was complete. I wasn't sure if I wanted to hand over the half of Akuma or hold onto it, they may take her into custody, and she was conniving enough to figure out how to restore herself if she had the chance but then they might just destroy her.

Until I could figure out what I was going to do with her, I set the carrier down in the bushes, making sure the lock was on it strong enough and double checking to make sure the tape was still covering her mouth. I knew the clones were strong enough to destroy the lock. I walked down to the others standing behind Micheal.

"Did they find Akuma?" I whispered.

"No, she seems to have disappeared somewhere with my brother." Stopping for a moment, Micheal looked back at me.

The officer came over when he saw me talking to my brother. He had files in his hand as he looked like he had a lot of questions.

"Her notes make absolutely no sense. We did find dig sites and there were several bodies buried. You were said to have been last with her. Where is she?" He asked.

"It was taking you a long time to get back here when I messaged that she came back. She was trying to kill me, but her clone got in the way, and she fell into the orange water acid and dissolved, it turns out she wasn't a true twin but a clone. If you follow the clear path back that way you will see the cabin. She's apparently been working on it for a while, she was obsessed with me until she found out she wasn't going to have what she wanted. She's the one who killed her own sister, or rather

I should say the original single child, but her parents passed them off as twins." I stated.

"Do you have proof she's a clone? What am I saying, no one is going to believe me that there are clones. There are tons of people here that look identical but that means they are related, and I can't explain how unless they are several sets of twins that simply are close genetically." He seemed extremely confused.

"Then let me demonstrate for you and it will clear a lot up for you." I called one of the clones over to stand in front of me.

I knew I had to be fast since I doubt, they would let me do this to a person if they thought they were real. And I understood being skeptical over clones, it wasn't something that was normal. Placing my hand on his shoulder and the other on his arm, I pulled his arm off. The shirt he was wearing tore with it. I was thankful I was strong, but I could have sworn the officer was going to throw up. Several others came over quickly with their guns drawn ready to stop me from further injuring the person. The chief of police made his way to the front of everyone.

"He just tore his arm off; we'll need an ambulance up here right away." He stated.

"We don't. He's not real and if he was a true human being he would be bleeding which this one isn't, he also doesn't show or feel pain." I slid the shirt sleeve off to show there were no bones, blood or veins that a human would have.

"Your positive she's dead, no coming back to kill anymore? Otherwise, she would have to face trial and more likely be executed because of how many she killed." The chief said.

"She wasn't capable of emotion. Killing to her was no more different than survival. She had a goal in mind for some reason and was willing to do anything to achieve it, killing wasn't personal and she felt nothing from it, so she died the same way she was created. I want to make sure the toxic acid is destroyed properly so no more are made and she can't possibly return in anyway." I said.

"We'll collect the lab equipment she has in both of these places and take the clones with us; we'll find a way of destroying them." The chief stated.

"Do they have to be destroyed; they could be used to make up for the horrible things Akuma did." Skylar said.

"They are part of a murder investigation and considered tools of destruction and will be destroyed once there is a safe way to do so." He stated.

"A safe way is dropping them into the acid, it dissolves them." If they were going to destroy them then at least hopefully it could be quick.

"Are there anymore than the twelve hundred we found down there and, in the house, or the ones standing near you?" He asked.

"No, there were only the two places." I wasn't going to tell him any more information than I needed to, or they might raid and keep my parents' belongings even though they legally could own those.

"Do you know what happened to the ones in the hatch, they were waiting to be brought in but once our officer had a vehicle large enough to bring them all in, they were gone." He looked skeptical at me.

"Akuma told me she had to collect something from there and these were the ones from there. I assumed she would take them if you were not. I wasn't aware they were being held as part of this since those were not involved in anything other than being created by her." I said plainly.

"If you know anything else, don't hesitate to call me. I'll be checking on you since I don't know if this will be enough to close this investigation." He said sternly.

"We were victims in this, so we are all ready to go to our homes, both Skylar and I have pets we miss, and no doubt need care. That and I miss taking a hot shower, this has been rather traumatic for all of us. We don't mind answering questions or assisting, after all we are the ones who found out about this and led the authorities to it once we should, if we start getting blamed for any of this, you're going to need some serious proof. For now, you know where we live, but if we are not being held, I want to go home and shower." I wasn't happy he kept trying to blame us for all of this.

Not having a vehicle and no one was willing to offer us a ride, the three of us walked along the pathway home, over the bridge and down past the beach and the long road that usually we parked our cars on the side of the road. Micheal went on his way home, I walked Skylar back to hers which I could hear Taffy barking from inside. I was curious what mess the cat and dog would have made in my home.

Going inside I admit, it smelled. Both animals were fine, the pillows were shredded, and they had the smallest amount of food. At least they were smart, and it was going to take me a while to clean up, they used the fenced in backyard for going outside to go potty whenever they wanted. Filling their bowls freshly with food and water, the last thing I felt like doing was cleaning right now. I gathered the mess from the inside and tossed it in the trash.

I hadn't planned on taking a shower quite yet, instead I found my black clothing, I intended on going back and getting the pet carrier and hopefully they didn't find her. I also hid a file that showed all her locations, until I knew they were done with the investigation, I wasn't going to risk going to our parents' cabin where we were hiding. Eventually I would fill both Skylar and Micheal on what I was planning, but was thankful they were always willing to work with me by not questioning me when I said those were her only two locations. Either they didn't want to admit to the one with the pit and elevator into a space she had already cleared out herself or they genuinely didn't know about it.

Otis sat closer but still out of range so I couldn't pet him, the dog was incredibly excited about my being back greeting me enthusiastically. I felt incredibly impatient, in case I was being watched I kept the curtains drawn or they would have seen me pace back and forth. Later when the sun went down, I hadn't bothered to take my car either. I walked through the woods doing my best not to draw attention to myself. The only area I would be visible would be the bridge going across, watching around for a few minutes, I made a dash for it and went to the other side.

The pet carrier was still hidden inside the bushes, peeking in, she was still there, even though she didn't show expression, I could swear she was frowning at me no doubt wondering if I was going to come back for her or not. Careful not to be watched, I made my way back to my house until I heard a voice.

"Taking the cat for a midnight stroll?" He asked.

"You scared the crap out of me, no wonder why they assume you did something." I was slightly shaking.

"I was always good at sneaking up and scaring people. When the chief and us used to play hide and seek, I scared him rather well, maybe that's why he would like to pin this on me. He has five people watching my place right now." Micheal stated almost proud of himself.

"Did they follow you here?" I was surprised he got past them.

"It's not the greatest group. But at least they knew I was aware they were not good at hiding. I instructed the pizza delivery person where to deliver the pizza I bought for them. I don't need them passing out on my property from not eating. Right now, I have sex videos playing on my computer with a mannequin sitting on the couch. I should probably get back, but I knew you were up to something, which, by the way, I was right." Micheal always did know when I was hiding something.

"I don't want to risk saying right now, we'll carry on as normal, Skylar starts her job tomorrow, you do your usual thing and so will I. In a few weeks when they realize they won't find anything, I'll explain at the cabin." I hoped Micheal knew I trusted him but didn't like words being said out loud or they have a tendency to be heard.

"Not a problem, it will give me a chance to mess with my watchers, at least I'll be safe, just let me know if you're collecting cats. You don't need to be that guy." Micheal said.

"Just because you don't have animals doesn't mean I don't need to. I fail to see the downside of having too many of anything. But quick question, you don't have any of the clones at your place?" I was curious since he had picked out two.

"No, I don't, I left those at the cabin which was a good thing since I know they've gone through my cabin searching. I have them on video." Micheal stated.

"If they are still watching you tomorrow, let me know. They don't have any right to search your place when you're not there, they need a search warrant to do that. That's a personal move because he doesn't like you, not that you earned it. Tomorrow plan on going to the bar like we always did for drinks. I'll invite Skylar." Giving a nod of my head, Micheal took off as I went into my place.

Since Akuma didn't need air to breathe, I opened my large safe and placed the carrier in there. I wasn't going to risk taking her out. Closing the safe, I felt it was best she was in there in case they searched my place, it was an area they couldn't get to. Then I put the file I had in the safe below the floorboards for safe keeping. I could have put them in the safe with Akuma, but I wasn't going to risk that. I took every precaution to keep them apart.

At least I slept well, and Micheal having his house was being watched, no one was going to attempt to break into it. We met Skylar at the bar the next day, she was excited to talk about her new job, how well it was going and Micheal filled her in on his having fun with his watchers outside. They were outside the bar as well as a couple sitting near our table which we didn't care about since we were not worried what we spoke of. The sheriff joined his men at the side table when I waved over to him to join us.

"Do you have something you need to declare?" He asked as he stood by Micheal.

"Yes, I do, we have a recording of your men breaking and entering Micheal's place searching it without a search warrant. You obviously found nothing. I was the main target by Akuma, she didn't even feel Micheal was worth attacking or bothering her time with, yet your personal hate for him is the only reason you are wasting time watching him waiting for any tiny little thing, its harassment." I stated.

"Do you have this recording?" He sounded nervous.

"Yes, I have it written down for you so you can watch it online. It's not only recorded but also shared, emailed and on several thumb drives not in our houses in case you feel like breaking the law again. You can't claim it was when you thought we were missing, it was dated so we know it was after we willingly showed you where she was located, at least where her lab and everything else was." I made it clear I wasn't going to back down and he couldn't destroy it as if it was the only copy, we had.

"I realize it sucks not to have a body to show for who did all of that, its horrendous and unfortunately doesn't leave closure for those who need it. But honestly, everyone around town knows how kind, compassionate, prankster and horny Micheal is, he's been around long enough that everyone knows he would never do anything like that, I get you want to catch someone but if you try to pin this on him, you're stopping the truth from being out and the real culprit from being caught. Whatever happened to her sister?" Skylar asked.

"We can't exactly disclose any of that information." The chief coughed and walked away from us.

The other officers followed along with him. The next few weeks there wasn't anyone watching our places and things seemed to calm down, no more news since nothing else was showing up. No more updates on the victims keeping a lot of that silent.

# Chapter Twenty

It had been a few months since we came back. Skylar went on vacation first, then Micheal left, and I followed shortly afterward. We started to spend every weekend at the cabin, at first, we kept Akuma safely locked up and away from any clones so she would never have any chance at taking over again. We were much less trusting of others and careful in case they were ever interested in watching us again. It took a while to visit all the locations that Akuma had her laboratories built, not only to collect her clones but also any equipment, files and anything associated with her and the clones. We stored all of it at the pit where we first were taken to after the original party where all of it changed for us.

Akuma hadn't proved helpful at all, at this point her main goal was now to kill me, Micheal and Skylar. We were no longer her goal; she still couldn't show any emotion or difference of what was right or wrong. We found that with several of the clones who were upgraded, when they did something wrong, there was no correcting them. The reasoning ability couldn't be upgraded into them. I had gone back to college to learn what my parents had spent so many years developing. Over the next few years, we fought with those who were violent like Akuma, very few seemed balanced, but it wasn't something we wanted to risk exposing to the world yet. It wasn't something we were giving up on yet, there was so much potential, and we did use many of the clones to help fix things, volunteer when needed but for the most part, we spent time as a family, figuring things out, enjoying life and not worried so much.

We decided it wasn't safe to keep Akuma around anymore and even though she would never fully understand why, we told her it was more for her crimes and any possible ones she could commit in the future. She refused to work with us, so we dissolved her along with several other clones, lowering the numbers to something we could manage better.

We kept three main clones. Micheal picked his out a while ago, Skylar kept my duplicate and I kept Nova, there was something about her that was different, but then she was the only one who had DNA mixed from myself and the original Eisheth. We decided that it was certainly worth working with and hopefully completing it one day if it was ever safe, but we would be much more cautious than our parents had been.

After a few years passed, I was on my way to work when I found a sticky note stuck to my windshield. I held my breath as my heart dropped. Reading the note it said.

"Thank you for cleaning up my mess, when its time I'll come for you, and we can finish this."

www.ingramcontent.com/pod-product-compliance
Lightning Source LLC
Chambersburg PA
CBHW051254170626
46809CB00004B/1641

9 781939 985552